KINGPIN WIFEYS
SEASON 2
VOLUME 4

BY

K. ELLIOTT

November 2014

CONTENTS

KINGPIN WIFEYS II,
Part 1: A Dollar Before Sunset

Chapter 1

THERESA "TETE" MYERS WAS FORTY-FIVE YEARS OLD BUT LOOKED thirty-three. She was a physically fit woman even though she hated exercise, and she had the kind of genetics that allowed her to eat as much food as she wanted without ever reaching one hundred and forty pounds. She had a sculpted face with a button nose that she hated. Her hair was shoulder length and full of body. She was five foot six inches tall and she typically dressed conservatively. Her favorite designers were Tory Burch and Chanel. She was classy, elegant and sophisticated, but TeTe had not always been able to buy designer things.

TeTe came from very humble beginnings. She grew up in a trailer park in South Carolina with her grandmother and her twin sister. When the girls were eight years old, their mother was convicted of accessory to armed robbery and murder and given a life sentence.

With no one to take care of them, they had to go live with their grandma, whom they called Big Ma. Big Ma had birthed TeTe's mother, Lecia, at thirteen and Lecia birthed TeTe and Tessa at fourteen. As a result, her grandma was only twenty-seven years older than TeTe.

Big Ma was functionally illiterate and they were dirt poor. They couldn't even afford to buy coats in the winter. Everything that they received had come from the Salvation Army, thrift stores and yard sales.

All that started to change when the girls met a drug dealer named Slick, a tall skinny man with permed hair who always wore flashy designer suits. The irony of the situation was that Slick's brother was a preacher and they dressed exactly the same way. The girls were frequently picked up on the way to high school by Slick, and even though he was almost as old as Big Ma at the time, she didn't have a problem with him seeking out TeTe. They were poor and Slick helped them out.

He bought TeTe and Tessa clothes, jewelry and cars. Almost overnight, they had gone from being the lowlifes of town to being the town celebrities. All the girls wanted to be like them because they wore the best clothes, and all the men wanted them. Their hair looked the best because, while everybody else got their hair styled in town, Slick would take them to Charlotte and sometimes Atlanta.

But all the money and clothes that Slick had given TeTe didn't compare to the lessons that he'd taught her about how to make money. Slick was not only a dope dealer, he was also a pimp, and even though he made money selling cocaine, he loved being a pimp. He would always say, "Pussy has been selling since the beginning of time and it's going to sell to the end of time."

That thought always stuck with TeTe. TeTe had been one of Slick's women from the time she was sixteen until she was twenty-four. She was one of the four women that he called his wives and they were off-limits to everyone except him. The wives all knew that even though he could fuck around freely, they couldn't be caught with another man. Slick took care of them and they all had to do what he said or get cutoff financially.

Life was great until Slick got busted with four kilos of cocaine and charged with possession and white slavery. He received twenty years in prison. A year after Slick was gone, TeTe and Tessa were flat broke. TeTe sold their cars and moved to Atlanta. Tessa decided that she was going to go to school and become a nurse, but TeTe had bigger plans.

She would take what she learned from Slick and start an escort service. Over time, she became one of the most successful madams in the last twenty years. Her clients were rappers, music producers, politicians and businessmen. She even arranged international trips. One of her biggest clients was a Chinese businessman that was infatuated with Black and Hispanic women. She would send women to stay with him in Shanghai for a month at a time. Each time he called TeTe, she would charge him over two hundred grand—she loved those international calls. Being a madam had enabled her to live an amazing life of luxury cars, expensive jewelry and exotic vacations.

And today TeTe was celebrating her daughter Butterfly's eighth birthday.

• • •

Eight kids were invited to the birthday party. Four of them were Butterfly's cousins and the other four were random kids TeTe had invited. Butterfly didn't have any friends because she was a spoiled, pretentious brat. No kids ever wanted to be around Butterfly thanks to her mother.

Ever since she could talk, her mother had told her that she was special, and named her Butterfly.

The eight kids sang "Happy Birthday" to Butterfly as she sat at the head of the table. TeTe had declared her a princess for a day, so she wore a pink fairy princess costume with a tiara on her head. A three tiered, pink and white Chanel cake sat on the table about an arm's length away and some of the parents whispered among themselves that the cake was way too extravagant for a child. Luckily, TeTe didn't hear their grumblings because she would have definitely cursed them the fuck out in front of their kids.

Butterfly was her only child and TeTe dubbed her a miracle child since her doctor had told her she wouldn't be able to have children because of her uterine fibroids. And he'd been right until TeTe reached thirty-six years of age. A gangster named Tyrod impregnated her with Butterfly. Shortly after, Tyrod had been convicted on drug conspiracy and weapons charges and sentenced to fifteen years.

The doctor warned her that there might be complications and possible birth defects, but TeTe wanted a child and accepted the risks. TeTe's beautiful butterfly was born a healthy, eight pounds and one ounce baby girl.

TeTe had lived without a man for five years and primarily focused on her work until about a year ago when she met Eli, a man who was twelve years her junior. He made her feel alive again. She'd never thought she would like younger men, but Eli made her feel like she was in high school again and she figured why not have a younger man. She had money and a child, so there was nothing else she really needed from a man except companionship. Since it was okay for successful men to have a younger woman, she figured why not her? And that's where Eli came in. Eli only had three jobs—being her boy-toy, fucking her and making her happy. In return, she paid all his bills and let him drive around in her luxury cars.

When the kids finished singing "Happy Birthday", Butterfly successfully blew out the eight candles. TeTe told Eli to cut the cake and then told Butterfly and the kids to form a single line. The party guests all lined up with pink paper plates in hand waiting to get a piece of the delicious-looking Chanel cake.

Eli ran to the other side of the table with a knife in his hand, about to slice the birthday cake, when Butterfly stood up on the chair.

"I don't wanna cut my cake yet," she said, standing on her chair.

After all, she was the princess and she had the ridiculous tiara to prove it. She had a right to stand on the chair. This was her day—or so she thought.

TeTe approached her daughter and whispered, "If you don't sit your ass down. I'mma whoop your little ass right here in front of everybody."

Butterfly sat down in the chair with her bottom lip protruding.

TeTe said, "Why don't you want to eat your cake right now? All of your friends are standing in line for cake."

"Those ain't my friends," she pouted.

TeTe scanned around the room, observing the face of the parents and began to feel a little embarrassed.

Then Butterfly said, "I want to open my gifts first."

"Eli, we're going to open the gifts first, and then we can eat the damned cake," TeTe said, becoming angry.

The kids were still in line and TeTe instructed them to have a seat.

After they sat down, Eli brought the gifts to the table. Butterfly ripped into her gifts and discovered she had gotten some dolls, a bicycle and gift cards to Justice, her favorite store. She seemed unimpressed with it all because she didn't offer so much as a hint of a smile. When she ripped into the last gift that Eli had brought her, a Samsung tablet, all the kids at the table were impressed.

"Wow," one kid said.

Another said, "Man, that tablet is awesome. I want one for my birthday."

Butterfly stared at the tablet for about three seconds before slamming it hard on the floor, shattering the screen to pieces.

"This ain't no iPad!" she said as she began to cry. "I asked for an iPad and this is what you got me?" Then she looked at TeTe and said, "How did you allow this to happen?"

TeTe yanked Butterfly's little ass up by her arm. Her tiara toppled and crashed on the floor. She dragged her into the living room and closed the door.

"Don't you embarrass me in here!" TeTe said. "I'm trying my best not to tear yo' ass up in here on your birthday, you ungrateful little heifer!"

The child looked up at TeTe, terrified, although she was a spoiled little brat, she knew not to push her mom too far or she would get her ass thrashed.

"I'm a good mom and I try to do whatever you want me to do," TeTe said. "I never had half the shit you have when I was your age. You understand me?"

"But I'm never with you. I'm always with Auntie Lucille."

Auntie Lucille was Butterfly's nanny. Butterfly's comment made TeTe feel guilty because it was the truth. TeTe never spent a lot of time with Butterfly. She had to work and she didn't want her young daughter to ever find out what she did for a living. As far as young Butterfly knew, TeTe was a real estate agent. Butterfly actually told her teacher that and when the school asked TeTe to speak on career day and she had to declare that she was ill and send someone in her place.

TeTe called for Eli and he came running into the room.

"Didn't I tell you to get her an iPad?"

"You did."

"Well, why in the hell did you buy that piece of shit Samsung tablet?"

"I want an iPad," Butterfly said.

TeTe peeled off six one-hundred-dollar bills and said, "Go get the iPad."

Butterfly smiled brightly and said, "You're the best mom in the world."

TeTe was happy to hear that and she returned to the dining room with Butterfly trailing her.

TeTe approached the table and said, "We're going to cut the cake now."

The knife was lying on a paper plate in front of Eli's place. She went to get it and spotted a phone on the floor underneath the table where Eli had been sitting. She scooped the phone up from the floor. Eli had an iPhone and this was some kind of Android.

She held the phone up and asked, "Did anyone lose a phone?"

All the parents responded that they had their phones. Spoiled-ass Butterfly was the only kid there that owned a phone and hers was an iPhone.

It seemed strange that everyone had their phones and no one claimed this one. Eli was the only one that was gone, but he had his phone. She got one of the other parents to slice the cake, and she disappeared into the living room. She powered up the phone and scrolled through the contacts. Alisha. Vicki. Rakeeda. Monique. Brittany. Tiffany. Sharon. Shanel, Naomi. Brandy, Shanequa.

That motherfucker, Eli, had a secret cell phone with nothing but bitches names in it, TeTe thought. She thought his silly ass knew better but maybe he didn't know who he was fucking with. She told herself to remain calm as she checked for text messages. The last one was from some bitch named Brittany.

Brittany: *I miss you so much.*

Eli: *I miss you too, Bae.*

Brittany: *Why can't we be together?*

Eli: *We will be together. Just be patient.*

Brittany: *I've been patient for months, and you still with that old bitch. Is it because she has money?*

Eli: *I don't feel like arguing. I'm at Butterfly's birthday party.*

Brittany: *When you done eating your girl's old wrinkled pussy, come taste some young stuff.*

TeTe was furious. She went through each name and there were exchanges between Eli and each woman including naked pictures.

• • •

The next day Butterfly stood on a barstool and watched as Eli tossed goldfish into an aquarium filled with red belly piranhas, the most dangerous kind of piranhas in the world, vulnerable when alone but together they are unbeatable. The piranhas devoured the tiny fish. They were one of Butterfly's birthday gifts from TeTe. One of the piranhas was off in a corner and not able to get to the goldfish because of the other five.

Butterfly noticed. "Eli, see him in the corner?" she said.

Eli laughed and said, "How do you know that it's a he?"

"Huh?"

"How do you know that fish is a he?"

Butterfly smiled and said, "I don't know. I think these fish are boys because boys are mean."

Eli laughed and said, "Some girls are mean."

"But not like boys."

"Okay, what about him in the corner?"

"They ain't letting him eat."

"He's not aggressive enough. You got to be aggressive in this world if you want to eat."

"That's not fair. I want you to feed him. I want him to eat."

Eli stuck a metal pole into the water. The five aggressive fish went in the direction of the pole and Eli tossed a few fish to the piranha in the corner, making Butterfly smile.

TeTe entered the room without being noticed and flung the Android phone into the fish tank. Seconds later, the fish swam away from the pole and surrounded the phone.

Eli turned and said, "What was that?"

"That was your phone, motherfucker!"

Butterfly laughed and said, "Mommy threw a phone in the fish tank."

TeTe said, "I need you to go to your room right now. I got to talk to Eli about something."

Butterfly hopped off the chair and sprinted into her bedroom. Eli closed the tank and turned to TeTe.

"So, you have a secret phone?" TeTe said.

"Look, I can explain."

"What is there to explain? You're texting other bitches."

"That wasn't my phone."

"Eli don't lie. When you lie, you are just going to make it worse. Look, I need you to get your shit and go. Get the fuck out of my house. Right now."

"No."

"No, what?"

"I have nowhere to go."

"Go back to your mama's house."

"Look, I don't want to go. Please, let's talk about it. I'll do whatever you need me to do. I just don't want to go home. I want us to work. I love you. Look, I made a mistake, but I promise you, it won't happen again," Eli said as he thought about the comfortable life he had living with TeTe. He lived in a huge home, drove nice cars she gave him and he always had money thanks to her. This was the best he'd ever lived in his life and he didn't want to give that all up.

"Look, motherfucker, you really don't want to play with me. I will fucking hurt you!"

"I ain't playing with you. I love you. Look, I'm still young. I made a mistake, but I love you. Just think about when you were my age. You made some mistakes too."

"Look, motherfucker, it's not like you're twenty-five. You're thirty-three."

"I know and I'm embarrassed."

"You're embarrassed because you got caught."

"Maybe."

"Look, I feel like you're playing me, like I'm some goddamned sugar mama or something."

He grabbed her arm and pulled her into his chest. He started to rub her hair. "Don't feel like that."

"Who the fuck is Brittany?"

"Just some girl."

"She had a lot of shit to say about me. How does she know about me?"

"She saw us together before."

"My daughter likes you. That's the only reason I'm not going to make you leave. But please, don't play me again. If you do, it's not going to be pretty. I swear to you."

Chapter 2

BLACK'S COUSIN, BYRON, WAS IN TOWN FOR A COUPLE OF DAYS AND he wanted to shoot some hoops. He called Black and asked him if he wanted to come down to play. Black didn't like basketball and he wasn't any good at it but he wanted to get his mind off Lani so he agreed. Plus, it was a sunny fall day and he needed some exercise. Byron said that they were going to play some three on three and he needed Black to make up the team, if nothing else.

Black figured he'd go out there and work up a sweat, but he didn't want to go to the park alone. Ever since Kyrie had proven to be so disloyal, he didn't have many people he could trust. He called L and asked him to come along. L agreed and brought a .45 with him to keep the peace.

Byron was a tall, lanky with curly hair. He was biracial. His father was white, and his mother and Black's mother were sisters. He and Black were pretty close growing up, but after high school, Byron joined the Air Force and had been enlisted ever since. He now lived in Texas, and though he and Black were complete opposites, Byron still referred to Black as his favorite cousin.

Two lames named Tim and Scott, who had been Byron's high school buddies, were with Byron. Tim was in the Navy and Scott worked for Delta. Black knew both of them but they were not the type of dudes he would ever hangout with—Lames. Squares. Cornballs.

L showed up to the park, he was wearing a headband, wristbands, shorts, knee-high socks, Jordan High-Tops and a L's gut hung from a Nike

T-Shirt, small enough for a third grader.

"Damn, L, you look like you trying to play," Byron said.

"I thought that's why we were here."

Byron snickered at L's ridiculous outfit, but L didn't hear him. The cornballs wanted to laugh as well, but they knew not to. To them, L look liked the type of dude that would beat the fuck out of them, and if he couldn't beat them, they figured he didn't give a damn about shooting them. They had families. L's tattoo on his right arm declared, Nothing to Lose.

Black said, "L, I didn't know you could play."

"They called me Jordan in the pen." L snatched the ball from one of the cornballs and gave his version of a crossover. He ended up popping his knee and crashing to the court. He bounced back up, limping slightly.

"You okay, L?"

'Yeah, yeah. I'm okay. I just gotta get warmed up."

Black said, "L, you can play the first game."

Byron said, "I'll take L."

Black sat on the sideline and watched. He didn't want to play anyway so this worked for him. L scored eight points, so he wasn't a bad player at all, but he was terrible on defense. For a guy in his forties he could play, but it was obvious that he wasn't in the best of shape. Though he had huge muscles, his cardio sucked and midway through the game, L called a timeout. Everybody was confused. Was there something on the court that needed to be removed? Did he need to tie his shoe?

Byron said, "What did you call timeout for?"

L was slumped over, breathing like a bear. He glanced up at Byron. "Gotta catch my breath, man."

Everybody was laughing their asses off.

Black said, "We don't want my homie to have a heart attack."

After L caught his breath, he threw the ball back inbounds and they started playing again.

Moments later, two very masculine-looking trannies with long silky weaves, wearing pink and green AKA T-shirts along with pink spandex shorts, sat on the bleachers two rows behind Black. When Black noticed them, he scurried to another set of bleachers on the other side of the court. He would absolutely not be associated with any kind of homosexual activity.

The darker of the two trannies wore blue contacts. She stood up on the bleachers holding pink and white Pom-Poms in her hands.

She was about to go into cheerleader mode when she said, "Larry Harris."

L stopped dribbling the ball and one of the cornballs said, "Double dribble."

"I thought that was you, Larry," the smiling-ass tranny said. She dropped the Pom-Poms.

L saw her out of the corner of his eye, but pretended not to see her.

Black said, "L, do you know them?"

L didn't respond, instead he said, "Let's play ball."

"Oh, you are trying to act like you don't know me, Larry, but you know me. This me, Fy-Head."

The tranny's real name was Casey King, but in prison, they called him Fy-head as in Fire-head but since they were in the South, fire was pronounced Fy. Casey was given the name Fy-head because he would get some of the inmates off orally, and some even claimed that his mouth was better than a vagina.

The game started again as Fy-Head made her way over to the goal. She stood there with her hands on her hips. The hot, pink spandex shorts contrasted with her shiny black skin. Lumpy, silicone ass cheeks spilled from her shorts.

"Oh, motherfucker! You're going to act like you don't know me out here now? You didn't say that when we were in prison. Every motherfucking night you begging to eat my ass. Now, you going to act like you don't know me? Fuck you, Larry! You can act like you straight and shit, but I know the truth. I heard you had a baby, but that don't make you no man. I know what you really like. Fy-head knows the real you."

L called time-out again and approached Fy-head. He took hold of Fy-head's weave and flung her ass to the ground hard. Then, L took hold of Fy-head's puny neck and started to strangle the fuck out of her until the whites of Fy-head's eyes were showing. Fy-head gagged as L's hands held firmly around her throat. All L could think about at that moment was the girlfriend that he'd strangled to death for cheating on him.

"Let him go, L! You're going to kill him!" Black yelled.

Black sprinted to L's side and said, "L, it ain't worth it. Too many witnesses. Let him go, please? Do you wanna go back to prison?" Black took hold of L's arm and said again, "Let him go. It ain't worth it."

L released Fy-head's neck and she plummeted to the ground like a sack of apples. Fy-Head's partner sprang from the bleachers and charged toward L. By that time, Fy-head had bounced up from the ground and threw up her fists like she wanted to fight.

Fy-head's partner said, "We'll beat your ass."

Byron, Black and the Cornballs were laughing their asses off as Black led L to the bleachers and calmed him down.

L said, "I don't even know that motherfucker, and you know I don't play no homosexual games."

"I don't play no games either, motherfucker!" Fy-head called out. "None at all and if it's the last thing I do, Fy-Head is going to expose yo' ass. Me and you are the same, Larry, except you are in denial, motherfucker. But sooner or later, the truth is going to come out."

All the men at the basketball court watched Fy-Head and his partner sped off in a pink Honda. The word Barbie was plastered on the side of the car.

Chapter 3

JADA PHONED BLACK AND TOLD HIM THAT SHAMARI HAD TOLD HER TO pass some information along, and that they should meet somewhere to talk. They decided to meet at Houston's across from Lennox Mall. Black waited in front of the restaurant until Jada pulled up and handed the valet her keys. Jada wore a backless, black bodysuit that made her ass pop, new Indian-Remy, down to her ass. Chanel sunglasses shielding her eyes, and the Creed Spring Flower fragrance she wore lingered after she exited her car.

Some guy and his hood-rat were exiting the restaurant as Black and Jada were about to enter. The man turned and stole a glimpse of Jada's ass and the hood rat smacked the fuck out of him.

"Junior," the hood rat said, "you ain't about to be in here disrespecting me, motherfucker. All you think about is ass."

Black and Jada were laughing their asses off as the hostess led them to a booth in the back.

Jada ordered a glass of water with lemon and Black had some Grey Goose.

"I thought you were going to drink with me?" Black said.

"Trying to keep my alcohol to a minimum."

"Why?"

"Just getting older. I even got to start going to the gym."

"Keeping that body tight, huh?"

Just like the man with the hood-rat, Black had noticed her body too. If he didn't have so much respect for Shamari and Jada hadn't been one of Lani's friends, he would have smashed that ass.

The waitress placed the drinks on the table and said, "Ya'll ready to order?"

Jada said, "I'm not eating."

The waitress said, "You're not eating?"

Black detected hostility in her voice and said, "Calm down, little mama. I'll tip you good. We're just not hungry. Plus, I'll be ordering drinks."

The woman apologized. "I'm sorry, Sir. I'm just having a bad day." She disappeared to the kitchen.

"Damn, what the fuck was her problem?" Black said.

"Probably not making any money. You know how shit goes."

"I guess." Black sipped his drink. "So how is Mari?"

"He's fine. He's in USP Atlanta."

"Good, now you can go see him whenever."

"Yeah, that's good and bad. Good because he's my best friend but bad because you know how niggas in jail think you don't have a life."

"True." Black sipped his drink trying not to stare at Jada's tits but they were fascinating to him as he looked at her nipple ring prints pressing against her shirt.

She noticed him looking and blocked his view by placing her arm on the table.

"Does he need anything?"

"No. Actually he just wanted me to tell you that he appreciated what you did for him."

"Of course, Jada. I had to show them where the body was. I had to save his life if I could. I felt partly responsible for what happened."

"He knows you do, and he wanted me to tell you not to blame yourself. He said they were probably going to get him anyway, but if it's anybody's fault it was that faggot ass Craig."

"Who?"

"The doctor."

"What happened to him anyways?"

"I don't know. Who cares with his snitching ass, I don't ever want to see him again.

"Seriously Jada, I was too greedy I had money and I wanted to keep going. That was all my fault. He listened to me."

"Quit blaming yourself."

The waitress dropped the chips off at the table and Black ordered another drink. She brought it back quickly and after she was gone, Jada said, "We're going to have to get him out."

"What are you talking about? You want me to hire more lawyers."

""That or break him out."

"There is no way you're going to break somebody out of the Feds. Are you crazy?"

"Look, he told me to give you his connect's number and they would know what to do." Jada passed him the paper with the connect's name on it.

Black glanced at the paper. "Juan. 310-224-9090. He's Hispanic?"

"Mexican. Why?"

"So he's going to help me get Shamari out?"

"We don't know if he's going to get out, but we gotta try. And if we ain't able to get him out, at least you have the connect."

"Shamari told me his connect was black."

"He was at first, but we were buying so much product that time when we were out there with Imani, that we met the connect. The black guy was going to be leaving for county jail and he wanted us to meet the plug."

"So you know him too?"

"Yeah, I was the one who made the last run."

"Oh," Black said.

Jada could see that Black was deep in thought. She was hoping this clown wasn't thinking she was going to make any more drug runs because she wasn't.

"So what does he want for giving me the connect?"

"He wants out."

"But what if he can't get out?"

"Well, you have to take care of me."

"Huh."

"Huh, my ass, we just gave you the plug."

"I know, and I didn't mean it like that. You mean he wants me to give you money?"

"That's what take care of means."

"Oh, that's not an issue. I can do that."

"Look, right now I have money but that is going to run out soon," Jada lied. She hadn't spent one dime of the money that Shamari had left her because she'd been living off Big Papa.

"Look, I can do that."

"Good."

Chapter 4

Q'S NEW RESIDENCE WAS A PENTHOUSE IN SOVEREIGN BUCKHEAD. IT offered a panoramic view of Atlanta, had floor to ceiling glass, high ceilings and it was just marvelous. Starr entered the space and fell in love immediately. Q paced back and forth while she admired the place. Though he'd lived in a nice building back in Houston, this one, by far, was the most amazing. The amenities of the building included the Sky Terrace, a spa and a wine tasting room as well as a twenty-four-hour concierge service.

Starr said, "I love it. This place is amazing."

"Let me give you a tour," he said. They started in the kitchen and they ended with him showing her the private terrace that came with the penthouse.

When he was done showing her the place, Starr said, "Why so many bedrooms? It's just you."

Q led her to the bedroom across from the master bedroom and said, "I was thinking that we could make this T.J.'s room."

"What?" Starr laughed. "T.J. has a room."

Q looked at Starr. "I want you here with me."

"That can't happen."

"Why?"

"Because it can't right now."

"You know how I feel about you."

"I know Q, but—"

He gave her a quick peck on her lip and she liked it.

"But what? You don't think I'm a good guy? You don't think I'm attractive? I don't have enough money?"

"Stop it, damn it! Don't you ever say shit about money! I make my own money. I make enough money to take care of me and T.J. and that's all I need."

"That's not what I meant," Q said.

"I'm not one of your hoes you can pick up at the mall and dangle a few dollars in their face and have your way with."

"I know and that's what I like about you." He attempted to embrace her but she stepped back.

"Look, Q, I know you like me and I like you too, but what else is it than just like? Do I find you attractive? Hell, yeah! And I know you think I'm attractive."

"I think you fine as hell," Q said as he stared at her hips, ass and that tiny ass waist. He licked his lips.

"Okay, besides the obvious that we would probably have some bomb-ass sex, what else is there to this?"

"I don't understand."

"We have no history. You haven't taken me out or tried to get to know me or anything."

"Let's make memories together. Have you ever been to Greece?"

"I can't be bought."

He sighed. "I know you, Starr. I've known you for many years."

"You think you know me."

Q laughed and said, "I see. So I'm going from zero to one hundred?"

"Try zero to a thousand," she laughed.

"Take it down a notch?"

"Please do."

"Dinner tonight?"

"Yeah. Where?"

"My terrace. I'll get the chef to come over. And we can dine overlooking the Atlanta skyline. It'll be romantic."

"Well, I like to be romanced."

"I'm the guy for that."

Chapter 5

IT WAS A BEAUTIFUL DAY AND JADA HAD JUST LEFT THE CARWASH. Her Mercedes sparkled as she whipped it down Peachtree. She noticed the car behind her flicking its lights to get her attention. It was a nice looking guy driving a Tesla Roadster Sport. She thought to herself, that's original. Not many black men owned a Tesla. She had ridden in one before. Craig's partner had owned one and Craig had taken her for a spin once. She wasn't impressed with the car though. It was too pricey to be a car that was supposed to save money on fuel in her humble opinion. The guy in the Tesla blew his horn then he lowered his window and yelled out the window. "Hey, you in the Benz! Pull over, I wanna holla at you!"

Jada heard the clown, and she hoped that he didn't think that just because he was driving a nice car that she would pull over and talk to him. Hoped he didn't think that she was a Car-Ho, a woman that would give up the pussy simply because a motherfucker drove a nice car. She was not that kind of girl.

The idiot kept blowing and she kept ignoring his silly ass as she proceeded in the direction of Lennox Mall. She turned into the mall parking lot. She glanced into her rearview mirror and this stalker motherfucker was still following her. She drove her Benz right up to the valet and the stalker was right behind her. Jada sprang from the car and handed the valet the keys and started to approach the door. The stalker was following close behind. He watched Jada walk into the mall, his eyes on that tiny-ass waist and that 26-inch Remy swinging. She decided to try something different with her hair, and man, did long hair bring the boys to the yard. Not that she was looking for a man, but what girl didn't like attention and compliments? The attention that she'd gotten with the longer hair had been unreal.

The stalker said, "Miss Lady! Can I have a moment of your time?"

Though Jada was from the hood, she hated when ghetto-ass niggas approached her with that Miss-Lady shit. Jada turned to face him, and for the first time, she got a good look at him. He was a tall, average-looking dude with a full head of hair, and wearing Jordans. He did have a nice smile, though. She hoped that he would get to the goddamned point, but he just stood there looking silly as hell. His eyes occasionally glancing at her thighs.

Jada said, "Yes."

"I'm Eli."

"Nice to meet you, but I gotta be going."

"Where you headed?"

Jada turned to walk toward Bebe, walking bow-legged because she knew simple shit like that turned men on. "Bebe," she said.

"Bebe?" He said it like he had some disdain for Bebe.

"Yeah, what's wrong with Bebe? I'm just going to get this dress I saw before every chick in Atlanta get it."

"That's what I mean by Bebe. It's nothing special. See, if I was your man, we'd be in Lord and Taylor, Neiman, Gucci and Louis Vuitton."

Jada laughed because obviously this clown didn't know who in the hell he was talking to. She had so much in her closet that if she ever sold it all, she knew that she could buy a small house.

'"Yeah, if I was your man that Benz out there would be—"

"A Prius? You're just talking shit."

Eli flashed a wad of cash and Jada laughed. All thoughts of him possibly being legitimate just went out the window. He was a dope boy and a petty one at that. What real man over the age of twenty-five flashed money?

"Is that your trap money?"

She was a few steps away from Bebe, still walking bow-legged and throwing that ass a little bit harder.

Eli laughed, and said, "I'm a concert promoter."

"I'm sure." Jada stopped and turned to face him and said, "Look, that money don't impress me, especially if you ain't spending it on me." She smiled.

"Let's get out of here and go to Phipps."

"And what's in it for me if we go to Phipps?"

"A nice handbag or something."

"A handbag?" She laughed and said, "Do I look like one of those Instagram Thots that post pics of bags and shoes all day?" Actually, she'd just posted a picture of a new Chanel bag that Big Papa had bought for her, but this clown didn't need to know that.

"Hey, I'm just saying, you are too classy to be going to Bebe."

"First of all, there is nothing wrong with Bebe." She smiled and said, "Let me get my dress and I'll meet you at Phipps in front of the Louis Vuitton store. There is a bag that I saw that I wanted and then we can get some drinks."

• • •

Later that night, they were at the Whiskey Blue inside the W having conversation and drinks. Jada was happy. She had just gotten a new thirty-five hundred dollar Louis handbag from a man who was clearly not going to get any pussy.

Eli was smiling and grinning like he'd won the lottery. He was thinking of what the boys would say if they ever saw him with Jada. Although, in the back of his mind was TeTe. She would go the fuck off if word got back to her that he was out with another woman. His mind drifted back to the time she tried to stab him in the chest and the time she'd shot at him because she'd accused him of flirting with a woman at the grocery store. He would have to wrap this up quick.

Jada sipped her drink and asked. "So what do you really do for a living?"

"Concert promoter. I told you."

"Low-key dope boy."

"Why do you keep saying that?"

"Well, who throws money around like you, except athletes and dope boys?"

"What difference does it make?"

"None to me at all. All money spends the same."

"Exactly." He sipped his drink and took notice of her boobs. He decided that they were fake but still looked very delicious. He said, "Where's your man?"

"Who said I had one?"

"I mean look at you. There has to be someone special."

"He's in jail."

"Really?" He looked as if he wanted to ask for what but didn't want to be nosey.

"Drug conspiracy and murder. Life without parole."

"Sorry."

There was an awkward silence and then she asked, "So, who is the lucky lady?"

"Huh?" He'd heard exactly what she'd asked but was trying to decide whether he was going to answer the question truthfully or not.

"Do you have a woman?" Jada asked again.

"No."

"Why not?"

"Just don't have time for one, you know. I work all the time."

"Promoting concerts?"'

They both laughed.

"Yeah, promoting concerts."

He ordered another round of Patron and five minutes later another. Then he took another ten minutes after that. She watched him down shot after shot.

She said, "Damn, you drinking a lot, daddy."

"Daddy?"

"Just an expression. Don't take that shit too literal. It means nothing at this point."

His eyes were glassy and he was still staring at her boobs. He made his way to a chair beside her and placed his hand on her leg. She removed it.

"What's wrong, babe?"

"Nothing. You just need to slow down, mister." Jada had no intentions of fucking him today or ever. He simply wasn't her type. She figured that she would call him, flirt with him a bit and maybe get another bag or some jewelry out of him. She couldn't quite put her finger on it, but something about him was turning her the fuck off.

He ordered another shot, downed it and then excused himself and headed to the bathroom. On the way, he stumbled into a waitress, spilling a tray of drinks. The servers rushed to the scene to help the woman gather the broken glass.

Eli removed a couple of hundred dollars from his roll and tossed the money on the floor and said, "Sorry for knocking over the drinks."

Inside the bathroom, he pissed on his shoes for two minutes before realizing he'd missed the urinal. When he re-emerged from the bathroom, Jada noticed, and smelled, the pissy-ass shoes.

Jada looked at him and said, "It's time for you to go home."

Eli weaved haphazardly as they made their way to the valet parking.

"I can take you home and you can get your car tomorrow," Jada said.

"Where do you live?" Eli asked.

Jada laughed at his silly ass and said, "Oh, hell no. I didn't mean I was going to take you to my house."

He frowned and said, "I can drive myself home."

"You're wasted, man. You're going to kill somebody."

"I can drive, goddamn it."

The valet handed him the keys to the Tesla. He got inside and put the car in reverse and crashed into the car behind him. He parked the car and got out to see that there was no real damage. The owner of the car agreed. He and Eli shook hands and agreed not to call the police.

Eli passed Jada the keys and she asked, "Do you want me to drive you home?"

"Yes."

She got behind the wheels of the car but then Eli had second thoughts. TeTe would execute them both if Jada drove him home. There would be no way in the hell that he could explain to her that he wasn't fucking or at least trying to fuck Jada. She simply wouldn't believe it.

"No. Can you call me a cab?" Eli asked.

Jada used her phone and summoned an Uber driver. Two minutes later, the Uber driver came driving a red Prius.

Jada turned to Eli and said, "Here is your ride."

Eli said, "Have you lost your mind? I'm not getting in the car with a stranger."

"He's an Uber driver."

"What the hell is an Uber driver?"

Jada couldn't believe this motherfucker didn't know what an Uber was. "Uber is like a taxi service."

The driver said, "We're better and sometimes cheaper."

Eli looked at the harmless looking freckled faced twenty-something guy behind the wheel before staggering to the car and flopping down in the backseat.

The valet had just emerged with Jada's car when she realized that she still had Eli's keys and she didn't have his phone number. "Damn. What a goddamned dilemma."

She peeked inside his glove compartment and spotted a pile of cash along with the vehicle registration with an address. She decided to take the car to the address on the registration, drop it off and then come back to retrieve her car.

She called Starr. "Hey."

"I need a favor," Jada said.

"Yeah?"

"Can you follow me to this guy's house, so I can drop his car off?"

"I'll have to wake T.J. up to come."

"Oh, I don't want you to do that."

"It's no problem. He just went to bed and he's probably not asleep yet."

"I'm at the W."

"Give me twenty minutes."

T.J. was in the back seat asleep as Starr followed Jada to a subdivision called Cobblestone Manor in East County. The huge cobblestone home had a wraparound driveway. A Cayenne Porsche and a White Jaguar F Type sat in the driveway. Jada was about to leave when the light came on and a woman stepped outside wearing a white robe and a towel wrapped around her head. She appeared to be in her late thirties.

"Can I help you?" she asked.

"Well, I was just leaving Eli's car. He was drunk and he couldn't drive it home."

Damn, Jada was thinking. Maybe she shouldn't have bought the car home. This damn fool had a woman after all. She should have known his ass was lying.

"Where are the keys?" the woman asked.

"Under the armrest."

The woman examined Jada. Her eyes said, what does this bitch have on me?

"I didn't mean to cause any problems."

"What's your name? I'm TeTe." The woman extended her hands.

"Jada."

"You and Eli had drinks?"

"Yes."

"Where?"

"The W, downtown."

"Drinks, but no room?"

"Excuse me?"

"You had drinks in a hotel bar, but you didn't get a room?"

"I just met him."

"Never fucked on the first night?"

Jada ignored her silly-ass question. "I didn't know he had a woman."

"Look, Jada, don't even worry about it. I know you didn't know he had a woman, and that he didn't tell you. If you knew, you wouldn't have been bold enough to bring the car here, right?"

"Right."

TeTe removed her phone from her robe pocket and said, "Can I have your number, Jada?"

"Excuse me?"

"Look, Jada. You've been out with my man and I'm okay with that. I'm not one of those bitches that goes off on the other woman. He is the motherfucker that did wrong. I just need your number and I will call you to get your version of the story when he wakes up."

Jada said, "678-444-8999."

"Thank you, Jada."

"No problem."

Jada turned and sashayed away while TeTe studied her. She had an awesome body, but what else could she bring to the table. Jada didn't have shit on her as far as she was concerned.

Jada was about to step inside Starr's car before she called out to TeTe who was just stepping inside the house. "Hey, TeTe?"

"Yes?"

"There's money inside the glove compartment."

"Really?"

"Yes. I would hate for somebody to break in and take it. Although I don't see that happening in this gorgeous neighborhood."

"Thank you, Jada. You have been more than helpful."

Jada jumped in the car with Starr. Starr said, "Who was the woman?"

"Apparently his girlfriend."

"She didn't look too happy."

"I didn't know he had a woman. He lied to me. I just met him, but you're right, his ass is in trouble."

"You didn't like him, did you?"

"Not at all. In fact, I'd decided five minutes into meeting him that it wasn't going anywhere."

"How did you end up with his car?"

"Well, he offered to take me shopping. I accepted and after shopping, we had drinks. He got pissy drunk and he couldn't drive, so I offered to take him home. He declined and now I see why."

"How did he get home?"

"Uber."

"Damn! She is going to go off on his ass in the morning."

"And he didn't even get any ass. Damn homie!"

They both laughed their asses off.

Though Starr knew Jada had a history of fucking with married men, she believed her. Jada was bold but Starr knew that even she wouldn't be bold enough to come to another woman's house.

Chapter 6

STARR WAS WEARING A BACKLESS DRESS THAT GRIPPED HER ASS brilliantly when she arrived at Q's condo. Q lead her to the rooftop terrace and a server dressed in a white tuxedo jacket and black pants led Starr to the dinner table. The waiter pulled her chair out for her and helped her sit down. Q was dressed in jeans and Jordans with a T-shirt and an expensive watch.

"Drop dead gorgeous." said Q.

Starr was smiling hard. "This is very romantic, Quentin."

"Quentin?"

"Yeah, I'm not going to keep calling you Q."

"I like your accent."

'You trying to say I'm country?"

"No. Not at all."

"I was 'bout to say, you from Houston so you can't even call me country. Y'all are more country than us."

"I like Southern Belles."

"That's me all the way," Starr said.

"And that's what I like about you."

Starr made a sad face. "I thought you liked my ass?"

"Now that's what I love."

"Am I just an ass to you?"

"I can't win for losing."

She smiled. "Just kidding."

She was laughing hard as she stared at Quentin. Though he was older than what she was used too, he had a boyish appeal about him. She didn't even think about the fact he was almost forty. It didn't feel like she was with an old man.

The server came and poured a glass of Chardonnay.

Starr said, "This wine is cool, but can I get a Cosmopolitan?"

Q said to the server, "Can you get the lady a Cosmo?"

"Yes sir."

"Girl drink."

"I'm a girl."

"Yes you are."

"But don't get it twisted, I drink Hennessy too"

He laughed, "I know, that's what I like about you. I like real motherfuckers."

"The only way I know to be."

"So no wine for you tonight?"

"Right now, I want a Cosmo."

He was laughing his ass off and they locked eyes for a moment then he turned away. The server dropped the cocktail in front of Starr.

Starr sipped her drink and asked, "So, what's for dinner?"

"Italian."

"Italian is a broad term. What exactly?"

"Whatever you want, as long as it's Italian, we have it."

"I'll take some fettuccini and can I have some Calamari to get started?"

Q called the server and told him what they both wanted. The man disappeared into the kitchen and informed the chef.

Starr downed her drink and said, "Man, this terrace is awesome. If you don't mind me asking, how much does this place run you a month?"

"I paid two million for it."

"You paid for it straight up? No mortgage?"

"Yes. Why does that surprise you?"

"No reason. Just that Trey and I always rented. Trey never owned property."

"I know. That's one thing that I always tried to get Trey to see. I wanted him to own shit."

"But you know Trey never really had a legitimate job and his businesses were fronts."

"I know. I told him to buy into a franchise. That is one of the best ways to legitimize yourself. Me, I have several businesses from rental car services to laundromats to restaurants and real estate."

"Are they profitable?"

"Yeah, they're doing okay," Quentin said.

"So why are you still doing it, Quentin?"

"Doing what?"

The server appeared with another drink for Starr and as soon as he left,

Starr said, "Don't play dumb."

"Why am I supplying?"

"Hustling, supplying, dealing. It's all the same."

"Well, not exactly. I'm not out looking for customers. I have had the same ten guys for the past ten years."

Starr sipped her drink and said, "You've been supplying for ten years?"

"Yup."

"You must have tons of cash. I know you don't need to supply anymore."

Q's face became serious and he said, "I'm going to tell you something that I haven't told anyone."

Starr covered her ears and said, "I don't wanna know where your money is."

Q chuckled. "Well, I'm not going to tell you that. Not yet."

"Not ever," Starr said.

For the first time he noticed how nice her teeth and lips were. He wondered if she was a good kisser. Did she give good head? He just stared at her lips for a long time, wanting a kiss now but she was too far away. "What was I saying?"

"You said you were going to tell me something that you haven't told anyone, and I told you not to tell me."

He laughed again and said, "Oh yeah. Well, what I was going to tell you is that I don't know how much money I have. I really don't. I had ten million dollars five years ago. So who knows what it is now?"

"Do you ever worry? You must not sleep well at night."

"I sleep very well. Why do you say that?"

"You have that much money. Somebody has to know."

'Well, like I said. I've been dealing with the same guys for the past ten years."

"I don't think I can deal with another hustler...excuse me, supplier."

He laughed again.

"Seriously, Q. I'm a mom now."

"And I'm a father to four and T.J. makes five."

She smiled and his eyes zeroed in on her full lips. The moon was full and if he could steal a kiss, it would be amazing. The server brought the food and disappeared to get more drinks.

Starr bit into her fettuccini and said, "Q, you're a really nice guy but I don't think I could do it again. I got little T.J. counting on me. I have money saved and I'm making my own money. Plus there's the guilt I would have for fucking with you. You were Trey's friend."

Q stared at her. "Starr, Trey is not coming back. I hate to be so matter-of-fact, but he's gone. He's my brother and I loved him just as much as you did."

She dropped her fork and a tear rolled down her cheek. She didn't want to hear that Trey was gone and wasn't coming back, but it was the truth—he was gone and he wasn't coming back.

Q dragged his chair to her side of the table and rubbed her shoulders.

"I'm sorry," he said.

"No, it`s not your fault. You are just being truthful."

"So, there is no chance for me and you?"

"Not as long as you're playing that game."

"What if I quit?"

"Why would you?"

"Didn't I just tell you I have more money than I can count?"

"You'd really do that?"

They made eye contact as he rubbed her thighs and stared in her eyes and at those lips. "I would do anything for you. Anything."

She didn't know if he was lying or not, but it damn sure sounded good. He leaned into her and kissed her. She felt as though she was supposed to push him away, but she couldn't bring herself to do it.

Chapter 7

IT WAS ELEVEN A.M. AND ELI WAS SNORING LIKE HELL. HE WAS sprawled across the sofa wearing only his boxers when TeTe doused him with a bucket of ice water.

He swung his arms wildly and yelled, "Get the hell off me!"

He glanced up at TeTe standing above him, her hands resting on her hips. She was pissed the fuck off. He sat up on the sofa and TeTe stomped down hard on his big toe with her pink Nike running shoes.

"What the hell is your problem?"

"You're the one that came in last night drunk as fuck with piss all over your shoes. Where were you? And where the hell is my car?"

"What do you mean where is the car?"

"You didn't come home in the car."

"What do you mean I didn't come home in the car?" He chuckled. "Well, if I didn't come home in the car, how did I get home?"

"How in the fuck do I know? All I know is you stumbled your pissy ass in here last night and I told you that you weren't sleeping in my bed. You passed out on the floor, but you smelled so goddamn bad that I had Keon carry you to the sofa."

He sat up on the sofa. Trying to remember what had happened. Then he remembered Jada, the girl he'd met in the mall. They'd gone for drinks but he couldn't remember anything after that.

"That's an eighty thousand dollar car! Now tell me where the fuck is it?"

"Calm down. It's at the W on 14th. I was having some drinks with some guys in the lounge and I got drunk."

"That's obvious."

TeTe had her hands on her hips, just staring at his silly ass. She wanted to slap the fuck out of him for lying, but she would go along with him, play his little game. She had Todd, her enforcer, to take the car and put it in storage. She would make his ass pay for what the fuck he'd done to her. Nobody crossed her and nobody played with her heart. Those were the rules she'd set a long time ago.

"My car is at the W?"

"Yes."

"It better be because the insurance lapsed and if the car is not there, we are fucked," she lied.

"How did the insurance lapse?"

"Didn't pay the bill yet," she lied.

"You know you can track that car from an app right. Remember, the salesman told us so."

"I never activated the tracking device. You know I'm paranoid about people being able to track me. Something about that shit just ain't right to me."

"So you'd rather let an eighty thousand dollar car go like that?"

TeTe wanted to spit in that stupid motherfucker's face. "You're the one that let my car get stolen, not me."

"I'm just saying that there is so many things that you can do if you had been able to track the car. Remember, the salesman said that if someone had actually stole the car that you could lock it up from the app to stop someone from driving it."

"Fuck what the car salesman said. I want my car!"

He rose from the sofa, looking around for his other sock.

"If you're looking for your sock, it's outside with those pissy-ass shoes."

He was embarrassed but he was hoping like hell the car was still at the W. He knew there would be hell to pay if it was gone. Then he wondered where the fuck was his phone. Did he have Jada's number saved in there? No, he didn't remember getting a number from her. He didn't have that to worry about. He was sure that TeTe had investigated his phone. Although he had a code on his phone, he was sure that she would figure out a way to get inside the phone. Most women would. He spotted his phone wedged between two cushions.

TeTe said, "Look, you just better take yo' ass over there and bring my goddamned car back. I left eighty thousand dollars in the glove compartment."

"Eight or eighty thousand?"

"Eighty so that's an eighty thousand dollar car and eighty thousand in cash, motherfucker."

"Damn. I'll take a shower and go right over there."

Chapter 8

BLACK WAS STRAPPED FOR CASH BECAUSE OF THE RESTAURANTS he'd invested in. Though he knew his investments were for the best, he was the type of man that needed cash on hand at all times. He stared at the number of Shamari's connect that was scribbled on the piece of paper Jada had given to him. He didn't want to put the number in his phone. He was always leery about what he put in his phone, just in case he was ever apprehended. He didn't want to be linked to somebody that he knew absolutely nothing about. Who knows what kind of shit the connect was into? Perhaps they were connected to the cartel. You never knew what people were into. He appreciated Shamari keeping it real with him and passing the information along, but he just couldn't put Shamari's connect in his phone.

He didn't like to travel to buy drugs. He liked to buy his product in Atlanta, even if it was at a higher price than in Texas or California. He knew Jada knew the connect and he wondered if she would be willing make a trip for him. He called her and she answered right away.

"Hi, Black."

"I need to see you."

"For what?"

"I need a favor."

"Can't you ask me over the phone?"

"I'd rather we talk face to face."

"Is something wrong?"

"No." He paused. "Not at all."

"You know where I live?"

"The same place?"

"Where else am I going to go?"

"Give me twenty-five minutes."

"Ok."

Almost an hour later, Black arrived. Jada was just about to hop into her car.

"Damn, boy." Jada glanced at her watch. "Do you know what twenty-five minutes is?"

Black smiled. "Colored people's time, baby!"

Jada wasn't smiling. "That just means that you don't give a damn about somebody else's time."

"I'm sorry." He grinned again. "Take it easy, lil mama."

Black trailed Jada into the house. The lavender maxi dress made her figure look incredible. If Shamari wasn't his boy, he would definitely try to make a play for some of that ass. Then he wondered who was hitting that ass since Shamari was gone. Somebody had to be tapping it, that's for damn sure.

Once they were inside, Jada sat on the sofa and he sat across from her. Jada was waiting patiently and her facial expression looked as if she wanted to say hurry the fuck up. Talk.

Black scanned the room, buying time. Trying to figure out what he was going to say. There was an awkward silence and she noticed Black staring at her boobs. She covered her chest with her arms to let him know that she knew he was looking. She hoped his black ass didn't think he was going to sleep with her because that was not an option. She was nobody's Thot.

"What do you want?"

"I need a favor."

"I know."

"I'm low on money."

"Look, Black, I ain't got no money for you to borrow if that's what you think. I got the money Shamari left me, but I ain't fucking that up."

Black laughed and said, "No, that's not what I meant at all. I don't want your money, Jada."

"What the fuck is it then, Black? I ain't got all day. I got a nail appointment."

"Can you make a run for me?"

"What?"

"Can you go see the connect for me?"

Jada looked at him like he was damn idiot. Motherfucker had lost it. Who the fuck did he think she was? A mule? Sure, she'd done it for Shamari because she loved him, but she didn't give a fuck about Black. She knew that he never cared about anybody but Lani.

"Hell, no."

"I'll pay you good."

"Look, Black, Shamari told me to give you the number and that's what I did. I gave you the number."

Black kneeled and said, "Please, Jada. I need you more than anything right now. I know I can trust you."

"To be honest with you, Black, Shamari told me to give you the number but told me to limit my interaction with you. He said motherfuckers want to kill you. He didn't know what he would do if something happened to me."

"People been wanting to kill me all my life. Do I look like I'm afraid?"

"Look, Black, I can't do it. It's not like you want me to go across town. You want me to cross the country. That's not something I'm willing to do."

Black stood and hugged Jada. "Look, I appreciate you keeping it one hundred with me."

"That's the only way I know how to be."

• • •

Jada had just left her nail appointment when her phone rang. She didn't recognize the number but thought maybe it was Shamari having someone call for him, so she answered the phone.

"Hello?"

"Hey, Jada. This is TeTe."

"Who?"

"I met you last night. You brought my car home."

"What's his name's girlfriend?" She laughed and said, "I'm sorry. I really didn't know he had a woman. Even though he told me he didn't, I should have known cuz most dudes lie."

"Ain't that the truth."

"TeTe, how can I help you?"

"Look, if he calls you, tell him that you don't know where the car is. Don't tell him that you brought it home."

"He won't be calling me, TeTe. He didn't get my number."

"Really?"

"He got so drunk that he forgot to ask for it."

"Damn. One more thing, Jada."

"Yeah?"

"There was close to eighty thousand dollars in the glove compartment."

In a split second TeTe had pissed Jada off. "Wait a fucking minute, TeTe. I ain't steal a goddamn thing. Trust me. If I would have stolen something, you wouldn't have gotten any of the goddamned money back. Besides, I don't need your money. My man left me with plenty of money."

TeTe laughed and said, "I like you, Jada."

"You must not like me too much. You just accused me of taking your money."

"I didn't accuse you of anything. I just said I had close to eighty grand in the glove compartment."

"And how much was in there when you counted it after I gave you the car back?"

"Every penny. Every red cent and that's what I don't understand."

"What's not to understand?"

"Why did you not take the money? Most people would have taken something."

"Look, I'm no angel but I'm no thief. I didn't know that man that well but I appreciated what he'd bought for me. Do I trick? Yes, occasionally but I'm no thief. My mama ain't raise me that way."

TeTe said, "That was my money. Eli don't have a motherfucking thing. That's my car and that was my money and I appreciate you for being honest. And I want to give you something for bringing the money back cuz I really do appreciate it. Where are you now?"

"Buckhead."

"Let's link up."

"Look, TeTe, I don't need your money. You don't have to give me shit. I was just doing what I was supposed to do and that's not touch something that don't belong to me."

TeTe laughed and said, "I wanna give you five percent of the total. I can't help but think what if my eighty thousand dollars had stayed missing."

"Meet me at the Atlanta Fish Market on Pharr Road."

"It's going to take me about twenty-five minutes to get there," TeTe said. She hated the Atlanta Fish Market but she hated Houston's more. People spoke of these restaurants like they were the Palm or something. She always joked that Houston's was the Palm for black people.

TeTe drove up in her white Jag and valeted her car. Then she spotted Jada. She approached her and shook her hand. Jada was impressed with the older lady. Her skin was radiant and glowing. It looked like she had gotten some Botox but she was still beautiful and though she was older, she was very fit with a tiny waist. She looked as if she took very good care of herself.

The ladies were seated in the front of the restaurant.

Jada told the hostess that she would have the spinach and artichoke dip and a P-Diddy. She thought about Lani and how she loved that drink ever since Shakur had turned her onto it. She was sad for a moment. Damn, she missed Lani.

TeTe ordered a Tom Collins.

Jada said, "A man's drink?"

"Some people think I'm a man."

Jada looked at her suspiciously. After all, there were a lot of women in Atlanta that were former men.

TeTe laughed and said, "I was born a girl, Jada. Just like you. I just handle my business like a man."

"Oh."

TeTe dug into her purse and removed an envelope full of money and passed it to Jada.

"You don't have to give me this money."

"Look, I know I don't, but I appreciate what you done. You've proven to be trustworthy. I don't have a lot of people I can trust."

"Yeah, I damn sure don't know a lot of trustworthy people."

"You can trust me."

Jada studied TeTe's face as she wondered what the fuck she was talking about. What did she mean that she could trust her? She didn't even know this bitch, and besides, what woman tells another woman that she can trust her? Jada hoped TeTe didn't think that she would sleep with her. She'd have to be fucked up for that to happen with any woman.

"TeTe," Jada said and dipped her chip into some cheese before biting down hard into it. "Look, I don't know what your motivation is. I don't know you. I don't make friends that easy."

TeTe laughed. Jada was hilarious to her. She could tell a lot about Jada just by looking at her. She could tell she was a good person underneath that hard exterior.

"So you don't make friends easy?"

"No."

"What if I was a guy?"

"Huh?"

"Jada, I just gave you four grand. If I was a man and I gave you four grand, you mean to tell me that you wouldn't want to stay in touch with me?"

"Look, I don't do women unless I'm fucked up."

"I'm not trying to fuck you."

"What is the goddamned point of this conversation? What is your motive?"

"Jada, I just asked you a question." TeTe sipped her drink. "What if I was a man?"

"Are you calling me a gold-digger cuz you offered me money? I don't need your motherfuckin' money."

"Calm down."

"I'm calm, you don't want to see me when I'm not calm."

"This conversation is going in another direction."

"It's going in another direction because you're taking it in another direction," This old bitch didn't even know who she was fucking with. So many women have let the cute face fool them into underestimating her and so many have gotten beat the fuck down.

"Look, I'm not going to team up with you to try to trap your man in some bullshit," Jada said.

"Did I ask you to do that?"

"No, but what do you want from me?"

"Nothing. I just thought since you were loyal, maybe we can be friends."

"Friendships are earned, not given," Jada said, as she ate some more chips. "I don't make friends easy."

TeTe said, "My kind of bitch."

Jada stared at her and she couldn't figure what TeTe wanted from her if she didn't want to help catch her man up in some bullshit. Why would she want to be TeTe's friend?

Jada dug into her purse and offered her the money back. TeTe refused.

"How long has your man been locked up?"

Jada was dumbfounded. How in the hell did she know that Shamari was locked up? They'd never met or discussed him being locked up. She'd told Eli that her man was locked up. Maybe his bitch ass had told her. "Excuse me?"

"How long has he been locked up?"

"What makes you think he's locked up?"

"Earlier when we were talking, you said your man left you with plenty of money."

"But that doesn't mean that he's locked up."

"So am I wrong?"

Jada ignored her.

"Jada, tell me that I'm wrong?"

"You might be right."

"Look, you're high maintenance, Jada. I can tell you like rich men. I've been there and done that."

"Why are you telling me this? What do you want from me and why?"

"I just want your loyalty."

"I see."

"How long has he been locked up?"

"A few months."

"Is there anything I can do to help? I've got attorneys."

"He's fine. He's been sentenced already."

"What did they give him?"

"Life."

"He's not alright then."

"Look, I don't want to talk about it. I don't know you and why you need me."

"I left eighty thousand dollars in my car. Think about it. Who has that kind of money laying around?"

"Your man is a hustler, what else is new?"

"My man ain't shit. I make the money in my house."

When TeTe said that, it had become clear why Jada didn't like Eli. He was a pretender and that's what was turning her off about him. He just didn't seem like a Boss.

"So you're a hustler?"

"A business woman."

"But you don't know me. I could be a robber. I could be trying to get my man out of jail. I could be working for the feds."

"You're not and besides I'm not a drug dealer."

Jada wanted to ask what the fuck did she do to earn so much money but it wasn't her business. TeTe read her mind.

"I'm a madam."

"A madam?"

"You know what that is, right?"

"Of course. But why are you telling me this?"

"Because you looked like you wanted to ask me what I did, but I didn't want to pry."

Jada was silent and TeTe said, "Have you ever thought about getting paid to go on a date?"

"No."

"You've tricked."

"That's different."

"How?"

"It wasn't an arrangement."

"It was just an unspoken arrangement. I'm sure you've been out with a man and the only reason you were there was to get something out of him...like you were with Eli's dumb ass."

Jada laughed and said, "TeTe, I'm not going to be one of your hoes. I got money."

"It's not hoeing. Some of the men you don't even have to touch."

"I have money."

"One of my girls went to China for a month. The guy paid a hundred and fifty grand."

"What was her cut?"

"Fifty percent."

Jada thought that was great money but right now she had more money than she could use thanks to Shamari. And she always had Big Papa's fat ass to fall back on. "Look, TeTe. I'm not interested in it."

"Can we stay in touch?"

"Yes, you have my number. Call me anytime."

TeTe looked Jada straight in the eyes and said, "I'm a good judge of character, Jada. You're as loyal as they come."

"You know what they say about loyalty?"

"What do they say, honey?"

"Everybody's definition is different."

TeTe smiled. "I like that. I think I'm going to use that."

"Use it. I heard it from somebody myself."

They were silent for a moment then Jada said, "You probably thought Eli was loyal."

"Loyalty and faithfulness are two different things."

"True."

"You're right, though. He misled me and he's going to be dealt with."

Jada could tell that TeTe was not the kind of bitch that you crossed. She could tell she was very calculating and very observant.

Chapter 9

WHEN Q ENTERED STARR'S HOME. HE LOOKED AROUND AND SAID, "Where is T.J?"

"He's at school. Where else would he be at this time?"

"So how is he doing?"

Starr stared at the ceiling and said, "He has his good days and bad days. You know sometimes he asks about Trey. I peeked into his room one day and he was staring at a picture of him and Trey. He misses his parents a lot, but to his credit, he hasn't cried and he tells me he loves me and he's blessed for having me in his life." She stared at Q. "I can't let him down."

"Do you mind if I spend some time with him?"

"Yes, I do mind."

"Why?"

"Well he's had enough loss in his life."

"Nothing is going to happen to me." He brought her closer to him; his hand landed right above her waist and grazed her ass.

"Do you know how many times Trey said that to me?" She looked up at Q and their eyes met and held.

"I'm not Trey. I got enough money and I'm seriously going to leave the game alone." He released her.

"You know how many times I've heard that?"

"I'm on my way to Houston to tell my connect that I can't do it no more."

"Really?"

Q turned his back to her and said, "Yes. I mean I have enough money.

I want to invest in you." He faced her again and said. "I want us to be together and I know this is the only way I can get you to believe in me. Besides, I've lived my life. Now I want to live for my kids, including little T.J. I want to be a part of his life. You know how I felt about Trey."

"I know."

"I'm telling my connect that I'm done."

"How do you think it's going to go over?"

"Not too great. I made a million dollars a month for the last eight years. That was my profit. I can't imagine what they've made off me."

"You sure you want to do this?"

"If it means having you, I do. You're worth it."

She approached him and hugged him. "Be careful," she said.

He stared down at her. This would be the first time he had a real woman by his side and he knew that it was totally worth it. They kissed.

• • •

TeTe was sitting on her plush sofa toying with Butterfly's new iPad. That girl had a fit about the damn iPad and had barely touched it since they bought it for her. TeTe was looking for Hawaiian resorts on the net. It was time for a vacation and she'd heard that Hawaii was a great place to go. Some had called it paradise on earth. TeTe loved to travel. She wanted to see the entire world, but she knew that wouldn't be possible because of a felony assault and battery with attempt to kill charge that she had on her record. There were countries, like England and Canada, that simply wouldn't let her in, but she would visit the countries that she was allowed to visit. Eli tiptoed in and TeTe glanced over the tablet. She briefly made eye contact with his silly ass.

He sat down in an armchair across from her and looked as if he wanted to say something.

TeTe said, "Did you find the car?"

"No, I didn't. The hotel is going to pull the footage from the night I was there and see which valet I had given the car too."

"So you don't remember what you did with the car? You don't know where the car is? You don't know where my eighty grand is?"

"I don't. But I got twenty-five grand saved up. You can have it."

"You goddamned right I can have it. And you're going to work for free!"

"What?"

"I'm taking your pay until we find out something about the car."

TeTe gave Eli ten grand a month to accompany some of the girls to hotels to make sure that they were safe. He'd introduce himself to the clients and tried to get a good feel for them.

He wanted to tell her she was out of her goddamned mind, but he knew that she was crazy. He knew that she didn't take losses, and besides, how was he going to argue with her when it was him that had fucked up? He would have to deal with it.

"And there is no car?" TeTe asked.

"The hotel is going to let me know who got the car."

TeTe stood and approached him. She was so close she could smell the Listerine on his breath.

"So you let somebody drive my car?"

"No." He turned away.

"Let me find out you let some bitch drive my car."

Eli turned away, thinking of Jada and wondering where in the fuck the car was. He knew that if TeTe found out that another woman had driven the car, there would be hell to pay. The truth was that he had been so fucked up that he didn't know if he'd given the car to Jada or not and he didn't have her phone number or any other way to get in contact with her.

"So the hotel is going to let you look at the tape?"

"Yes. They should be calling soon to let me know what they saw."

"Who is going to be calling?"

"Security."

"Do you have a name that I can ask for?"

"Yeah, I mean No." Although Eli didn't know what the fuck was on that tape, there was no way he was going to let TeTe see it. He knew he'd fucked up by letting her know that a tape existed in the first place.

"So you don't know the name of the security officer with the tape or is there something that you don't want me to see?"

Eli just stood there looking stupid as hell. He didn't want to answer that question.

"Eli, what are you hiding?" TeTe asked.

"I ain't hiding shit. I'm just embarrassed that I was so drunk."

"I believe you're hiding something."

Eli turned and faced her. He wanted to come clean and tell her that he'd had drinks with a woman who stole the car. But TeTe was not a forgiving woman. He'd seen her pistol whip grown men while her goons held them down. She shot one man in the balls. She was not forgiving at all. He would have to take this information to the grave.

TeTe was smiling now and she said, "You know what? I don't even want to see the tape because you're going to pay me for the car, too."

"I'm going to get the car back."

"I don't care if you get it back or not. You're still going to pay for it, motherfucker."

Eli dropped his head. He'd been bitched by TeTe. He wasn't used to women talking to him like that, but then again, she wasn't no ordinary woman. TeTe was one of the most powerful crime bosses in Atlanta.

Chapter 10

AS SOON AS Q ARRIVED IN HOUSTON HE CALLED HIS PARTNER, Desmond Mackins, known in the streets of Houston as Fresh. Fresh was only thirty-one years old and was like a nephew to Q. Q had been partners with Fresh's uncle Kevin who had been killed at a nightclub about fourteen years ago. Fresh had been selling little packs of coke in southwest Houston ever since he was in high school. His connection was a Mexican American named Raul who was a couple of years older than Fresh and had attended the same high school. Fresh was happy making his sneaker money and he'd had a Benz in high school. In his mind, he was balling. One day, Raul approached him and said that his cousin Diego had five hundred kilos and asked him did he know anybody that wanted to buy some weight. The only person that Fresh knew with the money to buy weight was Q. He phoned Q and asked if he would be interested and Q said he was if the price was right. The price was much lower than Q was getting from his present connect, so Fresh introduced Q to Raul who then took Fresh and Q to Diego. Soon afterward, Q became one of the biggest suppliers in the southeastern United States and Fresh was his right hand man.

Fresh was an inch shorter than Q. He was stocky but not fat. He was solid muscle with dark brown skin and wavy hair. It was because of his hair that kids in his neighborhood had nicknamed him Fresh.

Fresh was talking on his cell phone as he entered Q's penthouse. Q sat patiently, listening to Fresh's conversation. He hated when people entered his home talking on the phone.

"Look, I'm telling you that wasn't me at Belvedere on Sunday night. You know how many niggas in Houston drive Bentleys?

He put the woman on speaker phone. Q could care less what this woman had to say.

"You love Belvedere's motherfucker. You love parking your car in the front of the club and I ain't seen but one white Bentley with blue tops."

Fresh pointed to the phone and whispered, "This bitch is crazy."

"Who the hell are you calling crazy?"

"I was saying this whole situation is crazy."

"You know how I felt with my friends calling me telling me you had that Thot in the car with you? And the bitch was supposed to be my friend."

"That wasn't me."

"I know it was you."

"Look, why am I even arguing with you. You broke up with me, remember?"

"But you don't go and fuck somebody. I know you know that ain't right. How would you like it if I fucked Q?"

Q was getting irritated listening to this conversation, and he said, "Tell her you will call her back later."

"Brandi, I'mma call you back later." He terminated the call.

He noticed that his partner wasn't in his usual jovial mood. His mood was much more serious than he'd ever seen.

"I want out," Q said.

"What do you mean you want out?"

"Can't do it no more."

"Why? What happened?"

"I'm tired. I'm too old for this. I'm almost forty years old. I've done this for over twenty years. I have enough money. Don't you know there's no retired drug dealers? They end up dead or in jail. You know that."

Fresh said, "I thought you were going to Atlanta to set up shop there. Instead, you come back and say you're quitting. Something happened and don't give me that 'I'm forty years old' bullshit, bruh."

"Look, man, I'm old and you're young."

"I'm not young and you're not old. You be killing me with that bullshit."

"How much money do you have?"

Fresh looked confused. "Less than you. Why?"

"You have enough money."

"Right now I do. Maybe."

Q said, "You got so much goddamned money that you don't even know how much you have."

"What's your point, bruh?"

"You got millions of dollars, but one life. It's time to live. I've had you under my wing ever since you were a kid. I love you like a nephew. Hell, like my little brother but we can't keep going, man. We just can't."

"You need a vacation, man. Why don't you go out of the country for a couple of weeks?"

Q's face looked sad as he was trying to explain that he wanted out of the game and his friend simply didn't understand.

"You've always wanted to go to Paris. Take one of your baby mama's with you."

"I'm seeing someone totally new."

"Really?"

"Well we haven't made it official."

"You remember Trey?"

"Trey from the A? I thought you said he got killed?"

"He did."

"What about him?"

"I'm seeing his ex."

"You're a cold motherfucker."

"Look, she's a good girl. He never treated her like she deserved."

"She has something to do with your decision, right?"

"Huh?"

"Your decision to get out of the game?"

"No...I mean..."

"You mean what?

"I'm a grown man."

"Pussy influences us all, you taught me that."

Q, deep in thought, turned his back to Fresh. Though he'd been thinking of getting out of the game, Fresh was right. It was Starr that was really influencing him. He knew that he couldn't be with her like he wanted to be with her. He wanted her to move in with him and he knew that there would be no way that she would want to move in with him if he kept dealing.

Fresh took hold of Q's shoulder and Q faced him.

"I support you, brother. I just don't know how Diego is going to take it."

Fresh and Q, along with a short man named Rico, who was a runner for Q and Fresh, were asked to meet Diego at a Mexican diner called Anna's in southwest Houston. They were led to a private room in the back of the restaurant. This is where Diego held most of his meetings. Anna was Diego's sister and she ran the restaurant. Diego was a compact man, close to fifty years old but in great shape. He was an ex-boxer and had dark greasy spiked hair and a graying goatee. Diego was followed by two cholos(Mexican Gang members) The cholos were dressed in khakis and wife-beaters. Tattoos, pledging their allegiance to God and Mexico, decorated their arms.

He smiled when he saw Q and Fresh. "Que'tal," he said.

Q replied and then said, "Speak English?"

"Espanol?"

"No."

The first time Q had met Diego, Diego was unaware that Q spoke Spanish so Diego had actually tried to cheat him. Diego was surprised when Q called him a tramposo. (A cheat in Spanish)

Diego replied, "Black Columbiana?"

And Q said, "Just a black man from Houston."

Diego laughed when he realized that he couldn't cheat him. They mostly did business in English, but every now and then Diego would get the urge to speak his native language.

"English, please."

"Espanol."

The men laughed then turned as Diego's sister Anna entered the room. Anna was a short woman with long hair that reached her voluptuous rear end. When she entered the room, every man in the room, besides Diego, watched her, lusting in amazement and appreciation over how the dress gripped that curvy body. She passed out bottles of water.

As Anna was leaving the room, Diego noticed that Rico, the runner, was still staring at Anna. Diego smacked the fuck out of him. He smacked Rico so hard that he tumbled out his chair.

Diego stood over him and said, "If you look at my sister like that again, I will shoot you in your goddamned balls, motherfucker!"

One of the goons, a man named Ramos, who had a muscular build and tats smothering his body and face, took hold of Diego's arms. "Easy, boss."

Diego looked at Ramos and said, "You get your goddamned hands off me! I know what I saw. I saw this man looking at my sister like he wanted to rape her. Goddamned pervert was looking at my daughter the last time you sent him to see me, Fresh."

He stood up and made his way in front of Fresh and said, "Why in the hell do you have perverts working for you?"

"We can trust him."

"Motherfucker is a predator. I know a predator when I see him."

Fresh wanted to say that every man in the room was looking at his sister's ass. Fresh had sisters of his own and it wasn't a big deal for men to look at them, but he knew Diego was different.

Rico picked himself up off the floor and Diego said, "You get the fuck out of here!"

Q ordered Rico to wait outside for him. Rico was holding onto his jaw and he stared at Diego. He actually thought that he could take Diego, but he knew that would be a mistake. He would surely die if he lifted a hand. As he was about to exit the restaurant, he saw Anna again and as badly as he wanted to steal another look at her ass, he looked straight ahead and got into Fresh's SUV.

Inside the restaurant, Diego said, "Do you want something to drink?"

"Water is fine." Q said.

"I'm talking about a real man's drink."

"Not right now."

"What is it that you want to talk about? Just so you know, I'm not going down on the prices again."

"Nobody asked you to." Fresh said.

"What is it then?

"Well, we won't be needing as much as we used to."

"Why?" Diego looked confused. "What are you talking about?"

"Q is retiring."

Diego laughed a wicked laugh and Q and Fresh stared at each other. Not really knowing what to make of the way he was laughing.

Diego turned to Ramos and said, "Q wants to retire."

Ramos started to laugh as well. Diego kept laughing and the other goon began laughing too. Then Q and Fresh started laughing at Diego.

Diego cracked his knuckles and approached Q. "You don't quit until I say you can quit."

Fresh and Q saw the cholos pull out their guns. Fresh removed his gun from his pocket and cocked it. If they were going to die, they wouldn't die alone. Fresh was going to take somebody with him.

Q stood. "Nobody tells me what the fuck I can and cannot do."

"You don't quit until I say you can quit."

"And I just told you, I do what the fuck I want to do."

Diego removed his button-down shirt and was standing in the middle of the private dining area with a wife-beater on. His biceps were bulging and one of the arms had a red and green tattoo of the Virgin de Guadalupe.

Anna burst into the room and asked, "What's going on?"

Diego said to his sister, "Get the hell out of here!"

Anna left the room and Diego gave Q an icy stare.

Q stood up and said, "So, you want to fight me?" He approached Diego and said, "If you wanna fight, we can fight."

"You don't want to fight me, Quentin, because I'm telling you, if you lose, I kill. Do you want to die?"

One eyebrow raised, he wasn't smiling. He was serious as hell. Q knew that if he wanted to make it out of there alive, fighting Diego was not the way to do it.

The room became silent and Fresh grabbed his partner and said, "Let's get out of here."

"Smart man."

As he was about to leave the private dining area, Diego yelled to Fresh, "I'll have another thousand kilos Monday. Five hundred for you and five hundred for your friend."

"Fuck you!" Q said.

"Have a nice day," Diego laughed. "Nobody quits around here."

Chapter 11

SASHA AND BLACK LAY NAKED IN THE BED. HER HEAD WAS ON HIS chest and he was staring at the ceiling fan when Sasha said, "Tell me about her."

Black was startled and he turned and faced her. "Huh?"

"Lani."

"What about her?"

Sasha turned to face him and sat up the bed. "You loved her?"

Black was uncomfortable with Sasha talking about Lani. There was a silence in the room. Black rubbed her leg not knowing how to answer the question.

"Did you love her?"

Black stared at her and said, "I did."

Sasha sighed. "Was she the only person you ever loved?"

"Besides my kids and my Nana? Yes."

"What made her so special?"

"She was like my home girl. Of course, I was attracted to her, but she was loyal and faithful to me almost to a fault and that's hard to find." Black paused. "I can go on for days about her good qualities, but what good is that going to do me. She's gone."

"Do you think about her?"

"All the time."

"You were thinking about her when you were staring at the ceiling a minute ago, weren't you?"

"Why do you say that?"
"I could just tell."
"Yeah."
"What were you thinking? Do you mind telling me?"
"Are you a therapist or something?"
"No."
"What difference would it make?"
"Well, I think it's always good to talk to someone."
There was another long pause and finally Black said, "You're right."
"What were you thinking, Black?"
"I was just thinking that we weren't on good terms when she got killed and that her mother thinks I had something to do with it."
"Really? Does it bother you that her mother thinks that you had something to do with it?"
"A little, but what really bothers me is that I never got a chance to talk to her before she died."
"Did you cry?"
"What kind of question is that?"
"Did you cry when Lani died?"
"I got a little misty eyed."
"I'm saying you need a good cry, Black. You need to get it all out. It will be good for you."
"Look, I've never really cried when someone died, except the one time when my auntie died and my Nana had to bury her. When Nana cried, I cried. Not because my auntie died, but because my Nana was in so much pain."
"But you're in pain now, Tyrann"
"I am and again there ain't a damn thing I can do about it."
"You need a good cry."
A single tear rolled down Black's face.
"Lani is gone. She loved you."
"She did."
Sasha held Black's hand and Black rested his head on her chest and cried like an infant.

• • •

Black's cell phone rang and when he looked down at it he realized that it was Big L.
"I got some info for you, my brother."
"What kind?"
"I know you don't like talking over the phone. Can we meet at Handle Bar?"
"It's going to take me about thirty minutes."
"Perfect."

L sat in the back of the restaurant at a table with a red and white checkerboard tablecloth eating a greasy-ass hamburger and fries when Black walked in. L spotted him and waved him over to the table. When Black sat down, he grabbed one of L's fries and chomped it down.

"So what was so important that you couldn't talk about it over the phone?"

"I know where Avant is."

"Who?"

"The snitch's cousin. The one that was with him when he killed your girl."

"Where and how do you know?"

"Man, this was totally a coincidence. I was playing poker at the gambling house over in Stone Mountain and he walked in. I didn't know who he was, but then he started popping shit about his rat-ass cousin, saying that he'd left him plenty of money and that everybody in there was a bunch of broke motherfuckers and losers and nobody had the money that he had. I wanted to smack the fuck out of him till I realized who he was. I tried calling you last night but your phone kept going to voicemail. I figured you were cupcaking with some broad."

"You sure it's him?"

"I'm positive."

"How?"

"I pulled him aside and asked him was his cousin named Kyrie. And he said, 'Yeah, how you know?' "

"I told him some shit about I used to hang out with Kyrie."

"He believed you?"

"How is he going to prove it? Kyrie ain't here to be telling I didn't." L grinned.

Black ate another fry and L stared at him. L didn't appreciate Black eating all his goddamned fries.

"I need to get him."

"Look, man, you say the word. I'll knock him off. Just tell me how much you're paying."

Black reached for another fry and L caught his goddamned hand. "Order your own."

Black laughed at L and looked at him like he was being petty but he knew that L was serious.

"Look, L, I don't need you to kill nobody. I want you to get him and bring him to me."

"Bring him to you? For what?"

"I got other plans for him. Just do what I say."

"For three stacks?"

Black dug into his pocket and counted out fifteen one-hundred-dollar bills. He presented them to L and when he reached for them, Black yanked the money back and said, "Can I have some fries?"

L laughed and pushed the whole plate to Black's side of the table.

Black handed him the money and said, "You'll get the other part of the money when you bring him to me."

Chapter 12

TETE WAS RESTING ON THE BED, NAKED EXCEPT FOR ONE OF ELI'S T-shirts, when Eli passed her a shopping bag that he'd proclaimed had the money that he owed her. She pinched the bag trying to gauge what was in the bag. She didn't know how much was in there, but she knew damn well it was nowhere close to the money he owed her.

"What the fuck is this?"

"Ten bands."

"It's a long way from eighty."

"Look, I'm doing the best I can."

"It ain't good enough."

"You're going to get every penny."

"And the car?"

Eli paced and avoided her eyes.

"Did you ever talk back to security?"

"Not since the other day. They were going to call the police but I told them that I thought a friend was playing a joke on me. I didn't want to answer all the questions about why I had the GPS deactivated. Then they would want to talk to you since the car is in your name. I know you didn't want to talk to them."

"I don't talk to police."

Eli plopped on the bed beside her.

There was silence for a moment before TeTe asked, "Eli, have you ever cheated on me?"

Eli looked her in the eye and told her a goddamned lie. "No, I've never cheated on you. I would never cheat on you." All the while thinking what was she expecting him to say, 'Yeah, I cheat on you all the time, especially, when you're out of town.' He could never tell her that. That would never go over well with her.

She smiled and he wondered why she was asking him that. Had she been to the hotel to get the tape? Maybe she had and maybe the tape showed him and Jada.

The remote control to her surround sound was lying on the nightstand beside the bed. She flicked it on and the Flawless remix by Beyoncé and Nicki Minaj came on.

She placed his hand underneath her T-shirt to her breast and said, "I'm glad you've been faithful."

He massaged her breast and she removed the T-shirt. "Bite my nipples," she said.

Eli removed his clothes and shoes then climbed into the bed with her and started sucking her nipples.

"Eli, bite them, goddamn it!" she said as she fingered herself.

He bit one nipple and ran his finger over the other one until it was erect and then he dove between her legs. She had a landing strip on her kitty. She didn't like hair but she was against being completely bald because it made her feel like an adolescent. It was odorless and she took pride in that.

He wouldn't fuck her. She hardly let him fuck her, but she enjoyed head and she liked Eli because he was so good at it. He sucked her inner thighs. He kissed her navel and she pushed his head down further until it reached her clit.

"Right there, Eli."

Eli licked her clit and she commanded him to suck it and he did exactly what she said as she rolled her hips. Eli didn't particularly like going down on her. He felt as if he was being degraded. Emasculated. He felt like he was the bitch and she was the man, but he did what he had to do because he'd never met a woman that was so goddamned powerful.

She slid from underneath him and he lay on his back, his head on a pillow. Her pussy juices dripping down into his goatee, she sat on his face and he licked her pussy until she exploded.

Chapter 13

I NEED SOME DICK, THE TEXT SAID.

It was from Asia, one of Black's baby mamas. He couldn't believe what he was reading. He hadn't sexed her in a very long time. She had once told him that he'd never in his life see her pussy again and he believed her because he'd tried several times and she had resisted. Ever since his son, Man-Man had been kidnapped, she had very little to do with him.

He texted back: *Quit playing with me, girl.*

An image came through. A picture of her using a pink vibrator to play with her vagina: *Does this look like I'm playing?*

Black: *What time do you want me to come over?*

Asia: *After ten, the kids will be asleep.*

Black: *Cool. :-).*

It was around 9:45 when Black exited the driveway. He'd showered and shaved and wore a new fragrance called Artisan by John Varvatos. Though he'd been with Asia plenty of times before, he wanted to look and smell amazing because he knew that she was breathtaking. She was one of the best-looking women that he'd ever been with and he'd once declared if she wasn't so goddamned crazy, he would be with her, but she was just too emotional for him. She was the kind of woman that would cry over the slightest thing. He thought she might be manic depressive but goddamn was she a freak, and for that reason, he'd stuck around long enough to have two kids by her. When he pulled out of the driveway, a silver Ford Fusion bolted pass his him almost crashing into his car. He blew his horn and yelled, "Fuck you!"

Another text came through: *The kids are asleep.*

Black: *I'm on my way.*

Another image came though of Asia lying on the bed wearing a yellow thong, showing her beautiful heart-shaped ass.

Black: *Stay in that position :-).*

Twenty minutes later, Black rang the doorbell then remembered he had left the condoms in the car. He had to get those. He didn't need no more children. He headed back to the car.

Asia opened the door and stepped out on the porch.

Black spotted her and said, "Go back inside and leave the door open. I have to get something out of the car."

She disappeared back inside. He grabbed the Magnums and a .380 handgun that was lying next to the condoms. He locked the door and leapt onto the porch. A car stopped in front of the house and blew the horn. Black eyeballed the two people in the car but he couldn't quite recognize their faces. He did notice that one of them had dreadlocks.

Black yelled out, "Yo!" And cocked his gun.

The car bolted away and Black realized that it was the same car that had been on his street earlier.

Black ducked inside the house and slammed the door. He walked toward the direction of the bedrooms. He peeked inside Man-Man's bedroom. The boy was sprawled across the bed in his spider-man pajamas, covers so disheveled as if he'd been in a fight. He looked like he could sleep through a hurricane. Black repositioned him and covered him with a blanket and kissed him on the forehead. Inside Tierany's bedroom. She was his little princess and he kissed her.

She woke up and said, "Daddy?" She was surprised. "Am I dreaming?"

"No, I'm here, baby."

She stared at him and Black felt so damn alive when he saw his reflection staring back at him. He didn't know for sure who those men were out there, but he knew that it was his duty as a man to protect his kids and that's what he intended to do. He had to somehow handle the issues that he had with Shakur and even Mike.

He kissed her again and she said, "I love you, Daddy." she then dozed off.

He kissed her once more and said, "I love you, Princess."

Black entered Asia's bedroom. She had a huge canopy bed with purple bedding and purple drapes. A chandelier was suspended over the bed. Black had always felt like he was in a tent when he slept in her bed. She was lying across the bed wearing nothing but that yellow thong.

"What took you so long?"

"Had to kiss the babies."

Black stripped down to his boxer shorts. He placed the condoms and the gun on the nightstand.

"What's the gun for?"

"You know I've been shot, and ever since I got shot, I don't leave my home without it."

Asia stared at the gun but didn't say anything. It really made no sense to argue with this fool. Besides she wanted some dick and she wanted it now. She stood and made her way over to the lights and dimmed them. Black watched her ass sway from side to side. Her hair cascaded down to her ass. Black didn't remember her hair being that long.

She sat on the bed and she said, "Come here."

He tiptoed to the other side of the bed and she removed his boxer shorts. She noticed that his dick was limp.

She frowned and said, "I don't turn you on no more?"

"Not true. You absolutely turn me on."

She smiled and stroked his dick as he stood in front of her. She kissed it and said, "As much as I hate to admit it, you're the only man that has fucked me right in a long time."

"I've heard that one plenty of times before."

She frowned again. "I'm sure you have. Thanks for reminding me why we're not together, Black."

He laughed a little.

"What's wrong, baby? Why ain't he hard?"

Black thought about the strange men in the silver Ford Fusion. They obviously knew where he lived, but more than that, they now knew where his babies lived. Black stared down at his lifeless dick and it was still embarrassingly limp.

Asia took him in her mouth and it came to life a little as Black stared down at her beautiful ass while she took his dick deep down her throat. She gave him sloppy oral sex with lots of spit and suddenly his dick came alive in her mouth, but it was still somewhat limp.

She removed her mouth from his penis, gave a sad face and said, "Something is wrong."

"Nothing is wrong."

She sat on the edge of the bed and said, "Nobody loves head as much as you do."

It was true. Black loved head. He loved sex. He wanted it all the time and every woman that had ever been with him knew that much about him.

"Tell me what's wrong?"

"Why do you wanna know?"

"You are the father of my children."

"I invested in a few restaurants?"

"Yeah, Nana mentioned it to me. How is that working out for you?"

"It's going pretty good. It's just that I don't have any cash."

"What do you mean?"

"All my money is tied up."

"I can't get no dick because you're thinking about how much cash you have?"

"No, it's not like that."

He leaned over and grabbed a handful of ass. She smacked his hands away.

"What's wrong?" he asked.

"I don't want you to feel like you have to fuck me. I can find somebody to fuck me, you know? I'm not an ugly girl. I'm not desperate."

She stood and walked across the room and undimmed the lights. Black's eyes were on that big pretty ass of hers. When she turned, she caught him staring and she was glad she had that effect on him, but he had killed the goddamned mood.

He said, "I want you to move."

"Why do you want me to move?"

"I just want you to move. I don't want my children growing up in this neighborhood."

"There is nothing wrong with this neighborhood. It's close to their school and my job."

"I don't give a damn. I want you to go somewhere else."

"Tyrann, what the fuck is going on? You come over here with a gun and then you don't want to fuck me. Tell me what's going on. Is somebody still after you?

Who is it?"

There was silence in the room and finally she said, "Answer me, Tyrann?"

Black had heard her but instead he focused on her naked body. He yanked that thong down and threw her over the bed, her ass in the air. He rammed his dick in her tight little asshole and began to fuck her hard. His balls slapped her ass cheeks and he yanked her hair.

"Don't do that," she said.

He covered her mouth and yanked her hair until her wig came flying off. Now he knew why he didn't remember her hair being that long. A damn wig. He held in his laughter, right now he had business to take care of. His dick embarrassed him and he never, ever wanted anybody to say that his dick didn't rise to any occasion. He was Bankhead Bo's son and that kind of shit would never be allowed.

• • •

The following night, Black was lying in his bed with a stripper named Bambi. He was sound asleep with his hand resting in the crease of her ass when his phone rang. He reached for it but couldn't find it so he sprang from the bed. Looking underneath the bed, he spotted the illumination from the phone. Who in the fuck was calling him at that time of night? Maybe it was Asia trying her best to reach him.

His arms weren't quite long enough to reach the phone. It stopped ringing but he wanted to know who it was. He thought about the men that had cruised by his house and later by his baby mama's house. He grabbed one of Bambi's heels and used it to pull the phone within reaching distance. The screen read, Missed call from L. He dialed the number right away.

"Wassup?"

"Good news."

"Talk to me."

"Let's meet."

"Just tell me."

"I got your Avant. He tied up and in the trunk of my car."

"And you wanna say all that over the phone?"

"You told me to tell you."

"Right."

Black eased into the guest bedroom. He didn't want to wake the stripper.

"Avant's with you?"

"Yeah."

"Come over here right now. Let's talk in person."

Though Black changed cell phones every two weeks, he didn't know how safe L's phone was. He wasn't about to discuss a kidnapping over the phone.

"Come over where? You know, I don't know where you live."

Black paced. L was right. Black had never told L where he lived because he never fully trusted L but he had to tell him now. Look L I live at—"

"Can you text it to me?"

"No."

"Why?"

"L, can you get a piece of paper and write it down?

"Ain't got no paper. Text me the address."

"Get some paper, L. And call me back." Black terminated the call. The last thing he needed was a text exchange to be used as evidence for a kidnapping.

The stripper entered the den and saw Black sitting on the sofa. She was shorter than Black usually liked them and she wasn't all that, but boy, could she ride a dick and for that reason alone, Black loved her. She was standing there, butt naked, smelling like Bath & Body Works Candy Apple body splash, a tattoo of a cobra snaking around her back, the cobra head right above her navel, its tongue pointing at her kitty.

She said, "Was that your girlfriend, baby?"

"Yeah," Black lied.

"Do I need to go home?"

"Yeah, actually, you do."

She said, "Cool. I need to hurry home, anyway. I wanted to take my son to school in the morning."

L called back and Black said to Bambi, "Could you excuse me for a minute?"

"Yeah." She left the room.

Black said, "You got the pen and paper?"

"Yeah. What's the address?"
Black said, "9565 Eden Ridge Lane."
"Where is that?"
"Cobb County."
"This fucking pen don't work, just text me the address."
"Okay."
"I'm in Stone Mountain, it's going to take me at least forty-five minutes to get there."
"Forty-five minutes?"
"Maybe an hour, man."
"Okay, see you then."

Chapter 14

AVANT WAS A TALL SLENDER MAN WITH A MOHAWK AND VERY LITTLE facial hair. His arms were tied behind his back when L escorted him into Black's house. After the door shut, Black slapped the fuck out of him with the butt of his .380.

Avant wanted to cover his mouth, but his hands were tied. Instead he uttered, "Please, don't kill me."

"You should have thought about that when you killed Lani."

"I didn't kill nobody. That was all on Kyrie."

"Where the fuck is Kyrie?" Black asked, knowing damn well that he and L and tied bricks to Kyrie's body and dumped him into Lake Oconee which is about an hour away from Atlanta but Avant didn't need to know that.

"I don't know, man. He's been missing for over a month. You know word on the street was that he was snitching. I don't know, somebody must have been after him. Maybe he took off. Honestly, I don't know where he is."

"Really?"

Black spit on Avant's forehead and the spit spiraled into his eyes and mouth.

Black approached him and they were now nose to nose. Black said, "You killed the only woman I ever loved."

"I swear to you, that wasn't my idea. It was Kyrie. You know he thought you would kill him if you ever found out that he was talking to the cops, and so he had me go with him."

"What the fuck you mean, he had you go along with him? You're a grown-ass man. You chose to go with him."

Avant was crying now. His tears were fusing with Black's saliva. Again, he said, "Please, don't kill me."

L said, "Let me blow this bitch's brains out."

"That's too easy. I don't want to blow his brains out. I wanna make him pay."

"What did you have in mind?"

"Follow me."

Black led L to a huge unfinished basement. There were no windows and the floor was gravel. The only way out was the entrance door. L sat Avant on the dirt floor. Avant's arms were still tied behind his back.

Black said, "Have you ever lost something that you loved more than your own life?"

Avant said, "I lost my two-year-old daughter Avante. Just last year. I'm sorry, Black. I really am."

"Strip the motherfucker."

L looked at Black, dumbfounded and wondered what the hell was Black going to do. He stripped Avant down to a pair of gay-ass neon green boxers.

"Out of the boxers."

Avant stood in the gravel, stripped butt-naked. His three inch, uncircumcised Vienna sausage was surrounded by a mound of disgusting public hair.

Black sprinted upstairs and returned with a pair of latex gloves, a toiletry bag and a cigarette lighter.

Avant screamed like a bitch when he saw the lighter.

Black slapped the fuck out him with the gun. "Shut the fuck up!"

"I know big-time D-Boys. I know niggas with big paper. Don't kill me and I'll show you where they live.

Black backhanded him again and said, "Do I look like I need to rob some D-Boys, nigga? Do I look like I'm broke?"

"No."

L nudged Black. Though he knew Black wasn't struggling, that didn't mean he didn't want to know the whereabouts of the rich dope boys.

Black said to L, "We'll get back to that later. Right now, I got more important business to take care of and that's getting even with this motherfucker."

Black, wearing the gloves, approached Avant and took hold of his sausage. Black tried to break that motherfucker off. Avante howled.

"Shut up or I'm going to pour gasoline on your ass and set it on fire!

Avant murmured but he didn't dare scream again. "God, please help me," he said.

Black approached him. He was so close to Avant that he could smell the man's shitty breath.

"I wanna know one thing."

"I don't know where Kyrie is."

"I didn't ask you that."

"What is it that you wanna know?"

"What were her last words? Did she think I had something to do with it?"

"I don't know."

"You don't know what? That she thought I had something to do with it or you don't know her last words?"

"I don't know either. I swear, man."

Black turned to L. "There's a gas station around the corner. Go get me a gallon of gas."

L proceeded to take the stairs and when he arrived to the top of the stairs, Black said, "As a matter-of-fact, forget the gas. There's two baseball bats in the garage. Go get them."

L came back with two Louisville sluggers and handed one to Black. Black swung the bat and tried to break Avant's goddamned kneecap.

Black pressed the gun against the side of Avant's head. "Her last words, motherfucker."

"I don't remember," Avant said. The truth was, he'd read her lips after she'd gotten shot but he knew that would only piss Black off more.

"You're going to tell me her last words or I'm going to crack you upside your goddamned head with this bat. Understand me?" Black growled.

"I don't remember."

L cocked his bat and was going to smash Avant's skull when Avant said, "I'll tell you what she said."

L lowered the bat.

Silence. Black stood there waiting anxiously for what Lani had to say.

"She said, 'I think I'm going to die,' " Avant said. "That was the last thing I heard. She was talking to somebody on the phone."

Black knew she must have been scared as hell and but he still didn't know if she died thinking that he'd had something to do with it. I guess he would never know that.

Black grabbed Avant by the balls and squeezed him as hard as he could. Avant couldn't contain himself. He screamed as Black snatched his pubic hairs out until there was nothing but raw flesh. His balls were bleeding and Black doused his balls with the alcohol he had taken from the toiletry bag. When Avant screamed, Black smashed Avant's other kneecap. The naked man curled up in a fetal position, begging for mercy.

Chapter 15

ELI RECEIVED A CALL FROM SECURITY TELLING HIM THEY WANTED him to come down to the W right away. He walked inside the security office one hour later. The security officers were a young, black dude named Davion, who was a student at Georgia State, and a blond chick named Megan.

Davion said, "So we have the tape and we're going to show you what happened that night. Have a seat." Davion then pointed to a small folding metal chair across from the desk and Megan presented him with the tape.

In the tape, Eli staggered and then climbed behind the wheel of the car. He threw the car in reverse and crashed into a car behind him. Seconds later, he exited from the car. He, Jada and the owner were examining the car. Eli apologized and they came to the conclusion that there was no real damage. Afterwards, he hopped into an Uber vehicle.

"Okay, what happened to my car?"

Megan said, "After you left, the woman you were with got into the car and drove away. As you can see, it's right there on the tape."

Eli said, "Yeah I see that. Who told her that she could do that?"

Davion said, "Look, you and her were seen in the lobby having drinks, so you must have known her."

"I just met her that day."

"At the hotel?" Davion asked as he looked at Eli skeptical as hell.

"No, I met her at the mall."

"And you wined her and dined her to get her to your room?"

"I didn't even have a room in the hotel."

"You didn't even hit, bruh?"

"No."

"Oh. But you gave a total stranger the keys to your car?"

"I was fucked up. Can you tell me how to get in touch with this woman?"

"You didn't get her number?"

"I told you, the last time I was here. I don't have her contact information."

"And there is no tracking device on that brand new car? That's unbelievable."

"Are you here to help me or question me?"

Davion eyed at Eli suspiciously. "Look, put yourself in my shoes. What would you think?"

"I know that it sounds like bullshit, but it's really not."

Megan interjected with her high-pitched voice that was annoying the hell out of Eli, "We spoke with the valet and they said that you gave them permission to give her the car."

"Really?"

Eli thought hard. He knew that this was possibly true, but how in the hell was he going to explain this to TeTe? That the car was possibly gone forever? He knew that he couldn't tell her that he had given Jada the car.

"We got good news though," Megan said.

Eli looked at this dumb bitch and wondered what in the hell could possibly be good about this. He stood waiting on this bimbo to tell him what she considered good news because all he knew was that he was going to have to pay TeTe for the car and the rest of the money he owed her. And there was no telling what else she was going to ask of him. She could be very vindictive.

"We also have the license plate of the car the girl drove when she came here to meet you."

"What is it?"

"We can't give you that unless you file a police report."

"No cops."

"Why not?"

"Look, I just don't want the police to be involved. I don't trust them. I have a lawsuit against the Atlanta Police department," Eli lied knowing damn well if he said a word to the police about anything, TeTe would disassociate herself from him.

The bimbo eyed her watch and said, "Lunchtime."

Davion said, "Go ahead. I can handle it from here."

She said to Eli, "Good luck to you, sir."

When the door was closed, Eli said to Davion, "Look, I gotta get that girl's tag number.

"Sorry, bruh. I can't do it."

Eli removed five hundred dollars from his wallet and said, "You still can't do it?"

Davion stared at the money before saying, "Give me another five hundred dollars and I'll introduce you to someone who can find her."

Eli peeled another five hundred dollars from his wad.

Davion, the security dude, had connected Eli with a Georgia State patrolman. The patrolman had wanted another five hundred dollars before he'd given Eli the address where Jada's Benz was registered. The house that the Benz was registered to was run down and it surprised Eli that a girl like Jada would live in such a run-down neighborhood. This had to be a mistake. He rang the bell and after about three attempts, it was obvious that the doorbell wasn't working. So he banged on the door. He was about to turn and walk away back to his car when he heard somebody yell, "Who the fuck is trying to beat down my goddamned door?"

"I'm Eli. Is Jada here?"

The door creaked and an older black woman opened the door. A skinny-ass drunk dude was barely visible behind the rotund woman given that she was blocking his thin ass.

Eli said, "I'm sorry, ma'am. I got the wrong house, obviously."

"Wait a fucking minute. You said you were looking for Jada?"

"You know Jada?"

"Know her?" Louise laughed. "I shitted her out."

"Huh?"

"I'm her mama, and who the fuck may you be?" Louise said.

Charles, the skinny drunk behind Louise, said, "Yeah, who the fuck may you be?"

Louise turned and said, "Charles, if you don't go somewhere and sit your drunk ass down!" Louise balled her fist up as if she was about to knock the shit out of Charles and he galloped away before she could hit him. Then Louise turned back to the stranger at her door, demanding to see her daughter and said, "So you looking for Jada?"

"Yeah."

"And who the fuck are you?"

"I'm her friend."

"If you was her friend, you would know that she don't live here. So you try telling me another lie."

"I'm not her friend."

Louise stood there her hands hips, growing impatient with this strange-ass man.

"My name is Eli."

"So?"

"Can you get in touch with Jada? She knows me."

"Where she know you from?"

"The mall."

"She gave you her number?"

"No."

"Something ain't adding up. Eli. You tell me you met her at the mall, and she ain't give you her number. How in the fuck did you get my address?"

"The police."

"Oh, hell the fuck, no! You're a cop? Charles, get my goddamn gun. I'm gonna put a ball in dis nigga's ass."

Charles handed Louise a tiny-ass .22.

She turned the gun on Charles and said, "I ought to shoot yo goddamned balls off, bringing me this damn toy gun. Go get my shotgun, nigga!"

Eli was making his way to the car and Louise said, "Hurry and bring me my goddamn gun foe' dis nigga get away."

Louise trailed Eli and Eli stopped. He said, "Call Jada. She's going to tell you that she knows me."

Louise removed her Obama phone from her pocket and dialed Jada who answered on the first ring.

"Hey, Ma."

"Jada Simone, it's some nigga over here tombout he met you at the mall."

"What's his name?"

"Eli."

"I don't know no Eli."

Charles trotted his skinny ass outside struggling to hold the shotgun He passed it to Louise.

She cocked the gun and said, "Don't nobody know you around here, nigga."

"Tell her we had drinks at the W downtown."

Jada heard him in the background, and said, "You know what, Ma. I do know him."

Louise lowered the gun and said, "You one lucky ass. I don't play about nobody fucking with my babies."

Jada said, "I'll be there in a half hour."

Louise and Charles were walking back to the house with Eli tailing them.

Louise said, "You can wait in your car. I don't like your demeanor."

Eli was looking confused. What had he done to her? The old bitch was clearly crazy but at least Jada was on her way. Eli went back and sat in his truck. Thirty minutes later, Jada arrived. Eli thought the bitch looked simply amazing. He'd almost forgotten how she looked. She was driving the same Benz that she had been driving when he met her.

She hopped out of the car and said, "So how did you know where my mom lives?"

"It was a task."

"Tell me how you got her address?"

"Tell me where the hell is my car?"

Jada was puzzled.

"My car? The car I was driving the night I met you," Eli said.

Jada thought about TeTe, and it was clear that she still hadn't told him that they'd met. It was also clear that she didn't tell him that she had brought the car back that night.

Eli said, "Where the fuck is my car, man?"

"First of all, I'm not a man, and secondly, you need to lower your goddamned voice because my mama will surely bust a cap in your ass. Try me."

"No, try me, bitch. I don't give a fuck about your mama or your drunk-ass daddy. I need to know where that car is."

Jada didn't want to be in the middle of him and TeTe's bullshit. She said, "I'm not telling you a motherfucking thing. You come over here and disrespect me and you expect me to help you? Boy bye!"

Eli sighed and thought this whole damn family was nuts. He knew that he wasn't scaring nobody over here so he decided to take a more diplomatic approach. "Can we talk?"

"We're talking."

Louise returned with the shotgun. "Jada Simone, is everythang okay?"

Jada turned to Louise and said, "Yeah, everything is fine, Ma."

Louise gave Eli a nasty look before making her way back inside the house.

"Tell me where the car is?"

"I took your car back to the address on the registration. My girlfriend followed me out there."

"I don't believe you."

"Well, I can tell you there was a white Jag in the wrap around driveway in Cobb County.

"Really? So did you take any money out of the glove compartment?"

"I don't steal, nigga."

Eli stood there looking stupid as fuck. TeTe had the car and she had it the whole time. What in the fuck was she trying to prove? It was obvious she was mad that he'd been pursuing Jada, but why did she lie about the car? Why was she making him pay money back?

Jada said, "Well, if you don't have any more questions for me, you can get the fuck out of my mama's driveway. I'm going inside."

Eli thanked Jada and drove away.

• • •

Eli spotted the Tesla as soon as he pulled into the driveway. He dashed into the house and TeTe was lying on the sofa, curled up like a kitten.

He said, "So you had the goddamned car the whole time? What kind of games are you playing with me, TeTe?"

She sat up on the sofa and didn't bother to respond to his silly ass.

"Why did you do that to me?" Eli asked.

"I did something to you? You're the one meeting bitches in the mall, taking them to the bar and splurging on them. While driving my car!"

"Am I going to get my money back?"

"What money?"

"The money you said that was stolen with the car."

TeTe approached him and placed her pointing finger on his forehead. "Let's get one motherfucking thing straight. You don't own a goddamn thing in this house. You have been given a free ride because you are down with the boss. I made you, motherfucker, you didn't make me."

"But that was money that I earned."

TeTe laughed as she walked back to the sofa. He was staring at her figure. She looked curvier than before. He'd figured she was wearing Spanx because he'd seen one lying on the bed a few days ago.

TeTe laughed as she curled back up on the couch like a kitten, "Eli, have a seat."

She'd gone from one hundred to zero. Now, she was calm while a few minutes ago, she was all in his face, screaming. He'd seen her do that a few times before and it was a normal occurrence. He didn't know for a fact, but he speculated that she had some sort of personality disorder.

He sat on the armchair. He was still mesmerized by how tiny the Spanx made her waist look smaller than it already was. He had to admit, the crazy bitch looked sexy.

"Eli, would you like to tell me what you had when you met me?"

"I didn't have much."

"Okay, you didn't have shit."

"Right."

"And after I took you in?"

Eli laughed. "Took me in? You act like I was at a homeless shelter. I had my own apartment."

"Please. That roach invested apartment? I'd rather stay in a homeless shelter than stay where you were."

"But I had a home."

"Answer the damned question."

She was shouting again. This Dr. Jekyll and Mr. Hyde bitch was looney.

"Look, you gave me money and a car and I appreciate living in this mansion."

"This is not a mansion."

"Well it's a mansion compared to where I'm from."

"Now when I said that, you had a problem with it."

"You made it seem like I lived in a garbage can."

"You ain't ever lived this good in your life."

"True."

"And you think you deserve some money?"

"You said the money was stolen and it wasn't."

"And you were running around playing me out with a bitch that had a concrete looking-ass. I'll admit she was cute, but why you want somebody with a hard-looking ass?"

"I didn't even get her number."

"Which makes you stupid. Tricking and didn't even get the number."

TeTe made Eli look dumber than he'd already felt.

He said, "Look, keep the money if you want to keep it."

He stood up and was about to leave when she leapt from the sofa like a cheetah and stepped in front of him. She placed her arms around him and said, "Don't leave me."

She leaned into him and kissed him. She smelled magnificent and Eli looked at her tiny-ass waist. They were arguing a few minutes ago, and now she was acting like she wanted to make love to him. This was nuts. His hands caressed her back and rubbed her ass. She could feel his dick come alive. She removed his pants and he stood there wearing his boxers. She sucked his balls through his underwear until his dick stiffened.

She removed her dress and the Spanx and said, "Fuck me, Eli. Fuck me as hard as you can."

Eli stood there dumbfounded, wondering if he was going to get his money. Wondering what was the purpose behind her shenanigans. Hiding the car? Pretending the money was stolen? He'd learned to expect anything from TeTe and weird as it may sound, he liked her.

He dropped his boxers and she hopped on top and rode him until he exploded.

Chapter 16

FRESH ARRIVED IN ATLANTA AT 7:45 AND HE CHECKED INTO THE Westin besides Lennox Mall. He called Q as soon as he checked in and they agreed to meet up an hour later. They met up at The Leaf Cigar Lounge in Midtown. Fresh had an Opus X Cigar and Q had something a little bit milder. He didn't want a strong aftertaste.

After he lit up, Fresh said, "Look, man, we got big goddamned problems."

"What kind?"

"I sent Rico over to get the work from Diego, and he never came back."

"What are you talking about, he didn't come back?"

"I spoke with him over the phone. He says he's okay."

"What the fuck is Diego trying to prove?"

"He sent a thousand kilos but they still have Rico."

"What the fuck does that have to do with me?"

Fresh puffed his cigars and said, "Don't you see? It has everything to do with you. Everything, man."

"How?"

"He wants you to keep working and he says that he's not going to let Rico go if you don't work."

"I feel for Rico, I do." Q took a toke from his cigar and coughed. "But I can't let nobody make me do shit I don't wanna do."

Fresh looked serious and he said, "I know you don't want to do it."

"Motherfucker, can't make us do shit. At least not me."

"That's your ego talking."

Q knew what Fresh was saying was right. He did want to get out of the game, but he knew that Rico's life was in danger. Realistically, all he had to do was make three phone calls and the thousand kilos would be gone.

"Get Diego on the phone right now."

Fresh dialed his number and passed the phone to Q.

Diego answered, "Hello?"

"You piece of shit," Q said into the phone.

"I tell you who's a piece of shit. You're a piece of shit. I take you out of Fifth Ward and I make you richer than your wildest imagination and this is the thanks I get? Fuck Diego, right? Well, it don't work like that. Fuck you, Q. Fuck you and if you want your friend back, you know what you gotta do."

"Fuck you."

"I better have my money," Diego said and terminated the call.

Fresh puffed his cigar, looking on as he waited for Q to tell him what happened.

"Where is the work?"

"Houston."

"Well see, that's the problem. I'm not in Houston."

"Have your people come to the H. I'll serve them. Simple."

"You know they're not going to come to Houston unless I'm there."

Fresh knew what Q said was true. Though all of Q's customers called him when they couldn't reach Q, they really felt better when Q was there. Not that they didn't trust Fresh, they'd just rather work with Q. That was the way it had always been. Fresh looked at his friend who was really troubled with what was going on.

Q's phone buzzed. It was a text from Starr: *What are you doing?*

Q: *At a cigar bar called Leaf with my friend, Fresh.*

Starr: *Fresh??*

Q: *My homie from Houston. Why don't you bring a friend out here?*

Starr: *Okay. I was a little bored since T.J. is with his grandma. I'll call my girlfriend Jada and see if she wants to come out. How does Fresh look?*

Q: *Well, all dudes are ugly to me but he's cool as hell. I raised him right.*

Starr: *Is that right?*

Q: *:-)*

Q introduced Starr to Fresh and then he shook Jada's hand as Starr introduced them. When Fresh laid his eyes on Jada, his mouth flew wide open.

"So, you're my new girlfriend," Fresh said, looking at Jada.

Jada laughed and said, "Is that so?"

Fresh looked Jada up and down, taking in her backless black dress that gripped her ass, her flawless skin and her hair that reached the top of her ass. He wanted to take her in the bathroom and eat her pussy right there in the bar. He looked at her finger and said, "What the fuck is wrong with these dudes in the A? Why ain't you married?"

"I don't know. You'll have to ask them."

"No, I'm asking you." Then he turned to Q and said, "We're going to have a double wedding, bruh. We gotta marry these two."

Starr and Jada were smiling hard as hell.

Jada said, "So why ain't you married? I know there are a million beautiful women in Houston."

"Houston girls are so full of themselves."

"It's funny. That's what Atlanta dudes say about us. I think every man just wants something different from what he's used too. Houston girls are not full of themselves. There are good women everywhere and there are sluts and gold diggers everywhere," Starr said.

Fresh turned to Jada and said, "You ain't no gold digger are you?"

Jada said, "How does the song go? I ain't saying I'm a gold digger, but I ain't dealing with no broke niggas."

Jada expected Fresh to frown but instead he smiled and gave her a high five. "Well, you ain't got to worry about that over here."

"Is that right?" Jada said.

"That's right."

Starr said to Q, "Our friends are ready to get married."

Jada was impressed with Fresh. He was tall and dark. Even though she'd been with Shamari and Craig, she actually preferred a dark man. Plus, his wavy hair was making her seasick. His hair looked amazing along with his smooth chocolate skin and girl eyelashes. Fresh was fine as hell in her book and he could damn sure get it. Tonight, if he wanted it.

Fresh said, "Do you smoke?"

"Yeah, I love cigars."

"What's your favorite?"

"5 Vegas Gold."

"That's what Q's smoking."

"Q has taste."

Starr said, "That's obvious."

Starr said, "Well, I'm not a smoker. So one of you professionals are going to have to help me."

Q ordered two 5 Vegas Gold cigars for Starr and Jada. The server came and cut the cigars for the ladies. Jada showed Starr how to smoke and after she got the hang of it, it was cool.

Q said, "So how long have you two been friends?"

"A little over a year. We'd known each other for a couple of years, but we became real friends this past year."

"Really? You two seem like you've known each other all your lives."

"Well, we had a connection through a mutual friend who was murdered. We both were like her sisters and when she died, we got closer. There's nothing I wouldn't do for Starr," Jada said.

"We're opposites, but we're like sisters. I have a sister and she has a sister but Jada has grown closer to me than my own sister. We didn't even like each other at first."

"Why not?" Q asked.

"We had to learn to respect each other's differences, and I learned that if Jada is your friend, she really is your friend. She'll do anything for you."

Fresh said, "My type of girl."

Q stood up and said, "Look, me and my baby is going to go to the table on the other side of the room."

Starr trailed Q to a table in the corner. When they were seated, Starr said, "I didn't know I was your baby."

"You know now."

"You didn't tell me your friend was coming to town."

"He just showed up."

"So who is Fresh to you?"

"A friend that I practically raised."

"He's still in the game right."

Q stared at Starr, he wanted to lie to her but there was no use. She was street smart. He was silent.

"Look, Q, you don't have to lie to me. My dad was in the game and you know I was with Trey. I grew up in the hood. I can spot a D-Boy."

"Look, I wasn't going to lie. I was just trying to think of a way to explain myself."

"No need to explain. You're a grown man. You can do whatever the hell you feel."

Starr looked at him irritated as hell. Who did he think she was? He could do whatever he wanted. He has so much money, he can't even count it all and he still wants to go out and risk his life for a few more coins. She'd made up her mind that she would not put herself through this again and she wouldn't bring him around T.J. until he left the game.

"This is cartel business, not to mention cholos. You don't understand. These people just don't let you quit."

"Cartel?"

"Yes, Mexican drug cartel."

"I see, but what are cholos?"

"Gangs, some are connected with the cartel."

"So you're afraid?"

"I'm not afraid of nobody." He stared at her intently. "I'm not afraid to die, but I have a family in Houston and other people that are close to me that have to stay there. If you ask me, am I afraid for their safety? The answer is yes."

"I see."

"Look, like I told you before, I went down there and I told them I was getting out. Me and the head guy, Diego, almost came to blows and now Fresh is here to tell me that they are going to hold onto our friend until we get rid of a thousand kilos."

"So, they've kidnapped your friend?"

"Yeah."

"Damn." Starr's cigar had burned out so she flagged the server down and had him re-light it.

Starr puffed her cigar like a pro. She was stressed. She could see this man cared about her and she was starting to like him. She just didn't know if she wanted to go down this road again with the excuses.

Chapter 17

JADA WAS TALKING TO SHAMARI ON THE PHONE IN HER CAR. WHEN she drove up to her house, she noticed there was a car in her driveway. When she got closer, she realized that it was Black waiting on her. What the fuck did he want?

Jada said to Shamari, "You're boy is waiting on me in my driveway."

"What are you talking about?"

"Black is here. He is waiting on me."

"Why is he there?"

"He came over the other day and I gave him the information that you told me to give him."

"Put him on the phone."

Jada sprang from the car and passed the phone to Black.

"Hello?"

"What's up, black-ass boy," Shamari said.

"Hey, man, how are you doing?"

"You know how it is in here."

"Yeah. Do you need anything?"

"Fuck you mean, do I need anything? I'm in prison. Of course."

"Well, I'll give Jada some money for you."

"Appreciate you, man."

"No problem. Email me sometimes," Black said.

"I didn't even know you had an email address," Shamari said. He wasn't trying to be funny, but he couldn't picture Black sitting down composing an email.

"Very funny. It's easy to remember. Thedarkone@yahoo.com"

"Got ya. I'll hit you up from time to time. I won't wear you out."

"Hit me up anytime. We're brothers. I'll leave Jada with the money."

"Cool."

The operator came on and said, "You have fifteen seconds remaining."

Black passed the phone back to Jada.

"Hit me up later tonight. I love you," Jada said.

"I love you, too."

After Jada terminated the call, she said, "So what brings you here."

"I want you to go over to Ms. Carolyn's house tonight."

"Why?"

"I'm coming over. She won't talk to me, but I got something to show her."

"How can I make her listen to you?"

"Look, I just need you to be there. I'm going to ring the bell. I just need you to open the door for me."

"And let you in that woman's house? She clearly don't want nothing to do with you."

"Please, Jada."

"What are you going to do?"

"I can't tell you."

"So you want me to open the door and let you in this woman's house, and you can't tell me?"

"Do you think I had something to do with Lani's death?"

"I said all along, you didn't have anything to do with her death."

"Well, you gotta trust me on this. I gotta make this right."

Jada stared at Black for a long time. She didn't even know why she was entertaining this fool, but she knew that Lani had a soft spot for Black as terrible as people thought he was.

"Look, I'll do it."

"And what about what I asked you about earlier."

"I'll only do something like that for my man. And you ain't him."

• • •

Black had purchased a steel cage and he and L forced Avant inside. They were basically holding him like an animal in the zoo. Avant had been trying to figure a way to get out of the cage when he complained to Black earlier that it was cold and he wanted to get his clothes back. Black laughed at his silly ass and turned the A.C. on, freezing his ass even more. Then Black threw him a towel.

"What in the hell am I going to do with this, Black?" Avant said.

Black said, "I have absolutely no idea, but it just seemed like the right thing to do."

Avant wanted to cry but instead he asked Black where was he going to go to the bathroom and Black handed him a plastic bucket.

"What about food?"

He passed him a big bag of Purina's Puppy Chow.

Avant said, "I ain't eating that shit."

He'd held true to his word until day number four. On day four, he tore into the bag and started chewing that disgusting-ass dog food, but it was keeping him alive. Then he asked for water and Black gave him a red party cup.

"Okay, where is the water?"

"What water?"

"What am I supposed to do with this if there is no water?"

"You're a smart guy. I'm sure you'll figure it out."

"Why don't you just kill me and get it over with?" he asked Black.

"Killing you would be too easy. You tortured my soul and now I'm going to do the same to you."

"Fuck you."

"I was going to give you some water."

"And you're not now?"

"I told you, you'd figure it out."

And on day number six he figured it out. He drank his own urine.

When Black entered the dungeon he asked, "How does piss taste?"

"Fuck you!"

"No, fuck you, motherfucker." Black opened up the cage and saw that he was almost out of dog food. "One more outburst like that and I won't feed your ass for a week."

Avant stared at Black. He really wanted to curse his punk ass out, but since it was obvious that Black wasn't going to kill him, he needed the dog food.

"How long are you going to keep me here?"

"What difference does it make?"

"My wife has probably filed a missing person's report."

This pissed Black the fuck off. He grabbed the baseball bat and his gun. He aimed the gun at Avant and ordered him to come to the entrance of the cage.

"Please, just kill me."

"I'm not going to kill you, but I'll bust a cap in yo ass. Now, come over here."

Avant made his way over to the cage. Black dropped the bat and then grabbed him by his throat. Black dragged him out of the cage. Avant wanted to fight back, but he was too weak from dehydration.

Black said, "What about Lani's family? You ever think about what you did to her family?"

"I was just saying that my wife is going to notice that I'm missing and call the police."

"You think I give a fuck about the police?"

"No."

Black choked the fuck out of Avant. Avant wanted to die, but Black was not about to satisfy him. He'd make him suffer for what he'd done to Lani. Black released him from his grip and made him get back in the cage.

Black turned and was about to leave when Avant said, "Why don't you just kill me, please. Kill me."

Black stood still on the step and glanced back at Avant. "That would be too easy."

"But you killed Kyrie. Why him and not me?"

Black made his way back down the stairs and said, "What the fuck did you say?"

Avant sensed that Black was pissed. "I ain't say shit."

"That's what the fuck I thought."

"Can I have a shower? The other day you said I could take a shower."

"I did?"

"Yeah, you did. You remember when you came down here and said it smelled like raw asshole?"

Black grinned and said, "I did, didn't I?"

"Yeah."

"I lied."

"That I didn't smell that bad?"

"Oh, hell no. You do smell like raw ass. I lied about letting you take a shower."

"That's fucked up, man."

"No, that's life."

Black left the basement and returned with a bucket of warm water, a towel to wash with, bar of Ivory soap and a towel to dry off with. "I had a change of heart. Wash yo stankin' ass."

Then he chucked him a half-used tube of toothpaste and said, "Yo breath smells a little pissy."

• • •

A couple of days later, Black came back to visit Avant. This time L was with him. "L is going to watch you and feed you. I have other shit I have to be doing. So L will be here all day with you."

Avant didn't particularly like L because L was the one that had brought his ass here in the first place, but he didn't think being in a basement for days on end alone was something that he could get used too. Being in that basement every day with no sort of entertainment and not seeing his son was making him crazy. He'd started to talk to himself.

He glanced at L. He was a humongous man with arms like tree trunks and huge boulder-like shoulders. He always looked like he was pissed off and always had a snarl on his face. Avant didn't know if having L there was a good idea or not, but sometimes Black didn't return for days. At least there would be someone to talk too sometimes. But he still wondered what in the hell were they going to do with him.

Chapter 18

ELI WAS ASLEEP ON THE BED, AFTER MAKING LOVE WITH TETE. SHE'D let him have her doggy-style, he'd put her in the buck and they ended the session with a reverse cowboy before he exploded inside her. Then she gave him some amazing head before he dozed. Today had been a good day until someone snatched his narrow ass off the bed. He woke up swinging.

When he opened his eyes, he recognized the two men right away—Todd the enforcer and his cousin Dank. When Dank was around it was always bad news. This usually meant that someone would disappear. While Todd was lean and mean Dank was huge in stature with braids. He was very unattractive and even though he wore braids, he was balding in the middle.

Eli said, "Put me down, motherfucker."

They didn't listen to him and Eli said, "What's going on?"

TeTe appeared and she said, "Eli, surely you don't think you're going to get to do whatever you feel like doing and there won't be any repercussions."

"What are you talking about?" Eli struggled, kicked and wiggled trying to break free from the men but they were too strong for him.

"Get your goddamned hands off me!" Eli yelled.

"Eli," TeTe laughed and said, "I make the rules."

"What's going on?"

"Loyalty. What else could it be about, Eli?"

"I'm the most loyal person you'll ever find and you know that."

TeTe grinned with a crazed look in her eyes. "I have to pay you back for what you did to me."

"What did I do? Tell me right now, what the fuck did I do?" Eli cried.

"Do I have to remind you about the bitch in the mall?"

"We've talked about that. We made up and we had sex many times since then."

"What the hell does that have to do with anything? I was horny, so I fucked you."

She laughed a wicked laugh and Eli struggled. He almost broke free, so Dank slammed his scrawny ass to the hardwood floor and they held him there so he could barely move. He kicked Dank's foot and Dank pressed down hard with his shoes.

"You scuffed up my motherfucking Js," Dank said.

Eli's head was pinned to the floor. TeTe walked into his vision.

"Pick him up and set him on the bed," she said.

Eli looked horrified. What was this crazy bitch going to do to him?

"You have your money and the car."

"What are you trying to say? Just because I have my car and money back, that makes it right what you done?

"I just made love to you.

"You mean, we just fucked, Eli, you don't love me. We haven't made love in a very long time because you don't love me. You love all those bitches in your little secret phone. We fucked. I mean really? Why would I deny myself some dick? Huh?"

"I never got Jada's number. She'll tell you. I can take you to her mother's house, right now."

"But you intended to get her number. And why would you want to go to her mother's house?"

Dank twisted Eli's arm so hard that his ligaments sounded like popcorn. Chills traveled down TeTe's body. She sat on the bed beside him.

"I was in love with you? Did you know that?" she said.

He avoided her eyes. He didn't know how to answer that question. Though they were together, he didn't know if they were in love. He never felt that they were in love.

"I was in love. I thought you were the one for me. Butterfly loves you too."

"And I love Butterfly. You know I treat that little girl like she's my own."

"How? I'm curious. How do you feel that you treat her like she's your own?"

"I buy her things. I took her to Six Flags."

"With my motherfuckin money."

"I know it's your money, but it's more about the time."

"You're not loyal. I think you would snitch on me if you had to save your own ass."

Eli was now crying. "No, I would never snitch. I would never tell on you or nobody else."

"You wanna die?"

"No."

"Tell me, why should I spare you?"

Eli laughed. Not because anything was funny but because he had to laugh to keep from crying. "You're not going to hurt me."

"You wanna try me?"

"You love me."

"I did," TeTe said. "Pick his ass up and follow me."

They followed her to the den on the second floor of the house where the piranha tank was.

"Put his goddamned hand in the fish tank," she said.

"The piranhas are not going to eat his finger. It needs to be bleeding. They want blood," Todd said.

TeTe said, "Simple. Chop the motherfucker off and toss it in there."

"You can't be serious."

"No, you can't be serious. You know that I'm crazy. Why would you try me like this?"

She disappeared and came back with a hatchet.

Eli's grew agitated and he pleaded, "Please, don't do it! Please!"

TeTe said, "You're lucky I don't cut your goddamned head off."

Todd slammed Eli's ass back on the floor and restrained him with a chokehold. Eli grappled with the two men, trying his best to pull his arm away. He simply wasn't going to give in, but it was two against one and both men were much stronger than him.

Dank said, "This motherfucker won't be still. It's going to be hard."

Eli said, "What do you think I'm going to do? Just sit here while you chop my finger off?"

He stared at TeTe and thought to himself, out of all the bitches in Atlanta that had their own money, why in the hell did he have to meet her? He regretted the day that he'd met her old ass. His mother had told him to get somebody that was his age or younger and ever since he'd started seeing her, life had been up and down—mostly down.

She was nice one minute, buying him things, taking him places he'd never been but when it was bad, it was very bad. She had temper tantrums where she would throw shit at him and now it had come to this. This had to be a bad nightmare. He struggled to catch his breath as he stared at the two goons that had him pinned down.

TeTe disappeared into her bedroom and came back carrying a chrome 9 .mm and pressed it up against his temple. "Your finger or your brains?"

"Why are you doing this?" Eli cried, a river of tears rolling down his face.

She cocked the hammer of the gun. Eli went still. Dank stretched his finger out as far as it could go and Todd struck Eli's finger at the knuckle. Blood sputtered from his finger but it was not a clean cut. A jagged part of his finger dangled from his hand and blood spewed.

Eli was hollering like hell. "Oh my God! My finger! My finger!"

Todd struck his hand again, this time severing the finger. Eli stared at his finger on the carpet and cried like a bitch.

TeTe slapped him with the gun and said, "I spared you."

Eli's finger was lying on the floor, a ring still on it. Todd scooped the finger up with a Kleenex and chucked it into the fish tank.

Eli was still on the floor, crying as he watched the piranhas huddle and play tug of war with his finger until they finally ripped it apart and devoured it, leaving a sea of crimson.

Chapter 19

BLACK ENTERED THE HOUSE AND MADE HIS WAY TO THE BASEMENT. He heard a buzzing sound and when he got to the bottom of the stairs, he saw L sitting on a chair clutching a gun, a McDonald's cup in the other hand and Avant kneeling at L's feet. Avant was filing the dead skin from L's crusty-ass feet. Every toenail was black and crusty with fungus underneath and the bottoms of his feet were hard and nasty looking.

Black said, "What the fuck is going on in here?"

L grinned and said, "Mani-pedis."

"What the hell do you mean, mani-pedis?" Black said.

Black wanted to laugh at the mere thought of such an imposing figure like L getting a mani-pedi, but this was the same dude that bashed someone's head in while he was in prison for changing the channel from soap operas.

"Look, I had some crust on my feet and thought that our friend here could help me out."

This was slavery to have anyone touch those ugly-ass feet. There were McDonald bags on the floor and there was one inside the cage.

Black said, "Why did you feed him McDonald's?"

"I told him if he was nice, I would give him some food."

Avant struggled to saw the crust off L's feet with something that resembled a cheese grater.

Black said, "I told you what to feed him, and it was not McDonald's."

"This was a reward for giving me a pedi."

Though Black couldn't argue against anybody that came near those hideous-ass feet needing to be compensated, L was not following orders.

Black said, "L, let me talk to you for a second."

L locked the cage and unplugged the cheese grater looking apparatus while Avant chomped down on his double cheeseburger. L followed Black upstairs. L was barefoot. The cuff of his pants was above his ankle, and tissue was between each toe like he'd gotten a real pedicure. When they reached the top of the stairs, Black said, "What the fuck are you doing, man?"

"Everything is under control."

"This McDonald's is some bullshit. This is not what I wanted."

"I told you, it's for the pedi," L said. He sipped his grape soda and then said, "Besides, if we're going to kill the motherfucker eventually, what difference does it make? Hell, they even give you a last meal on death row."

"Look, man, we're not here to be this dude's friend."

'I know my job. He's still here, ain't he?"

"Okay, he's still here, but I gave you orders on what to feed him," Black said.

Black glanced at L's feet again and then said, "I know what this is about. You're trying to butter him up to get info about the D-Boys that he knows. So you can go jack them."

"No, man. I haven't even thought of that," L lied. "Get your panties out of a bunch, bruh."

Black realized there was no point in arguing with L. He said, "Tie him up, we need to go somewhere."

"What do you mean tie him up? He's in a cage."

"He's going with us."

"He is? Okay, I'll go do that." L turned and made his direction to the stairs before doing an about face and asking, "Can I finish my pedi at least?"

"I don't give a fuck what you do, bruh."

Chapter 20

JADA TEXTED BLACK AND TOLD HIM THAT SHE WAS AT MS. CAROLYN'S house. Thirty minutes later, Black and L arrived with Avant hogtied in the back of L's car. Black rang the doorbell and Jada answered then let Black come inside the house.

Seconds later, Ms. Carolyn entered the living room, and when she saw Black, she said, "Didn't I tell you I don't ever want to see your black ass again?"

"Ms. Carolyn, can I say something?"

"No. Get away from here. I'm calling the police because I've told your ass over and over that I don't want to see you."

She turned and was making her way back to the room to get her cell phone when Jada stepped in front of her.

"Ms. Carolyn, just see what he has to say," she said.

Ms. Carolyn gave Jada an icy glare. "Get outta my way, chile."

"Ms. Carolyn, I honestly don't believe he had nothing to do with Lani's murder."

"Why do you say that?"

"I was on the phone with Lani, and Lani's last words was Mike had something to do with it."

"Who is Mike?"

"Chris's brother."

Black cut in. "I can't stand Mike's ass but he didn't have anything to do with it. I know who killed Lani."

Ms. Carolyn turned and faced Black. "Who killed my child?"

"Kyrie killed her. My old friend Kyrie killed her."

Ms. Carolyn stared at Jada, "Now see what I mean about he had something to do with it?"

"I did have something to do with it indirectly, but it was not my intention to hurt Lani," Black said, then he paused and looked Ms. Carolyn directly in her eyes. "I didn't know he was going to do this. I swear to you, I didn't know." Tears rolled down his face.

Jada held Ms. Carolyn's hand as she could see the pain in her face.

"I loved Lani as much as I love my own kids," Black said.

Ms. Carolyn said, "Tyrann, you know I buried a son a few years ago. How could you let this happen to my only child? My baby?"

"I know and if I could take it back, I would. If I could change places with Lani, I would, Ms. Carolyn. You don't know how much I think about her and to know that I was the cause of this is a living hell for me."

"So where is this Kyrie guy and why hasn't somebody called the police on him?"

"You don't wanna know where Kyrie is."

"Oh yes I do."

"Kyrie is in hell."

"What?"

"Just put it this way, he ain't breathing."

Ms. Carolyn and Jada looked at each other as if they didn't know what to believe. Black called L on the cell phone and seconds later, L dragged a hogtied and gagged Avant into Ms. Carolyn's house.

"What the hell?" Jada said.

"Who is this man, Tyrann?" Ms. Carolyn asked.

"This is Kyrie's cousin."

"What did he have to do with it?"

"He was the man with Kyrie."

"Tyrann, are you crazy? Get this man out of my house."

Black told L to remove the gag and L did exactly that.

Black said. "Apologize to this woman for killing her daughter." And then he slapped the fuck out of Avant.

"Tyrann, this is all good, but this is not going to bring Lani back."

Jada said, "Black, this is crazy."

"Call the police," Avant said. "Please, call the police." He knew that even though he was sure to go to prison, they weren't going to treat him as fucked up as Black had been treating him. They weren't going to torture him, that's for sure.

Black said, "Take his ass back out to the car, L."

L gagged him again and dragged his ass out to the car and stuffed him in.

"I loved Lani, Ms. Carolyn, and I know I can't bring her back. But I would never intentionally do anything to hurt her. It's my fault. I get that. If she hadn't been dealing with a dude like me, she would still be here. I'm sorry from the bottom of my heart that she's gone, and I know you're going to be mad at me for the rest of your life, but I needed to get this out. I needed you to hear me."

Ms. Carolyn stared at Black for a very long time. He certainly seemed sincere and then she said, "It's not all your fault, Tyrann. You were the man that she picked. She chose to be with you."

"It's one hundred percent my fault."

"Tyrann, you remember that day that I saw you riding through the neighborhood?"

"Yeah."

"What was that all about?"

"To be honest, I don't know what I was riding through for but I know it had nothing to do with her murder. That's on everything I love." Black looked like he was very sorry for what happened and Ms. Carolyn believed him.

"I forgive you."

Everyone was silent and finally Ms. Carolyn said, "Bring yo black behind over here and give me a hug."

Black approached her and hugged her.

Chapter 21

IT WAS 8 P.M. AND Q INVITED STARR OVER FOR WINE ON THE penthouse balcony. First, she was thinking, wine? What kind of man drinks wine? Trey certainly didn't drink wine. All the men she'd ever dealt with were a little on the thuggish side and she liked that. She knew that Q was a thug too, but he was also sophisticated. More sophisticated than Trey had ever been and she suspected that he was worldlier than Trey. He liked cigar bars and wine.

Trey liked sweatpants and sneakers most of the time, and while, Q wore sweat pants and sneakers sometimes, he was also comfortable in more fancy clothes. He definitely looked comfortable as he stood in front of her in tight white pants, a blazer and loafers. A few months ago, Starr would have called this outfit totally gay, but he was confident in it and just as masculine as ever.

This was new for her, but she had to admit, she liked it and as hard as she tried to fight it, she liked him too. He got a bottle of Italian wine.

"How did you start drinking wine?"

"There is a white guy in my building in Houston who always came over with wine. I really didn't like it at first, but then I found some that I did like. But I really don't know that much about wine. There is just some that I like."

"Really?"

"Yes. As a matter of fact, the bottle that we're drinking, he gave it to me as a gift."

"You're open-minded, I like that."

"I try to be."

Starr sipped the wine as she looked out into the Atlanta sky. It was a beautiful night, slightly humid and stars decorated the night sky. She had to admit that Q was very romantic and very manly. Though she thought about Trey every day, being with Q definitely eased her mind a lot. The way he looked at her, she could tell that he wanted her, and it wasn't that he just wanted her sexually, she could tell that he appreciated her. She kept looking out at the night sky while his eyes were on that backless, electric-blue dress and those Giuseppes that elevated her ass so nicely.

She loved the way he looked at her and she blushed when he said, "You look amazing tonight."

She turned and faced him, her wine in her hand. "Thanks."

"I got something for you."

"Not another gift."

"I appreciate you."

"Look, you can appreciate me without trying to buy me."

"I'm not trying to buy you." He smiled and he looked so boyish, almost innocent.

"Good, I can't be bought and I have my own money. It's not what you have of course, but it's enough for me and T.J."

"Shhhhhh." Q placed his finger over his lip and said, "Stop talking."

"Ok."

From behind his back, he brought a light-blue Tiffany's box.

"Tiffany's? Oh god, another Trey."

"What are you talking about?"

"Buying overpriced stuff."

"Open the box, woman."

She removed the box top to find a diamond tennis bracelet. He placed it on her arm and she kept looking at it smiling. Not wanting to know the ridiculous amount of money he paid for it because if she found out, she would surely give it back to him.

"Do you like it?"

"I love it. It's so beautiful." She removed it and attempted to give it back to him.

He didn't accept it. He frowned. "What's wrong?"

"I can't accept this."

"I don't take gifts back." He placed his hand underneath her face and turned her face to him. Their noses almost touched and he said, "I want you to be my lady and not just my girlfriend. I plan to spend the rest of my life with you until death do us part. I want you more than anything in this world. I want to be your provider and your protector. I want to meet your parents. I want everybody to know that I love you."

Did he say he loved her? She didn't know if she loved him. She liked him a lot, and right at this moment, more than she'd ever liked him. And as much as she hated to admit it, she was falling for him and she was falling fast. He placed the bracelet back on her arm and he stood behind her, his arms draped her as they stared out onto the Atlanta skyline.

• • •

The clock on the dash read 11:17 p.m. when Black spotted the car that had been following him. He turned down his street, raised the armrest and took possession of his gun. He was going to turn in his driveway and if they followed, he'd made up his mind that he was going to open up on their asses. He knew L was in the house. He called L, but there was no answer. He kept driving and the car was still behind him. When he turned into his driveway, the silver Ford Fusion shot pass him to the cul-de-sac and busted a U-turn then bolted pass his house. He opened the door and ran inside and banged on the guest bedroom door. No response. He opened the door. He saw L's shoes beside the bed but L was nowhere to be found. He called out L's name. No response. He then made his way toward the basement. L had to be down there with Avant. Where else could he be? When he got midway down the stairs, he heard the sound of a wild animal. More like a wounded dog. He wondered what L had going on.

"L?"

He didn't get an answer. The wild animal grunts were getting louder.

When Black reached the bottom of the step, he heard L say, "Call me daddy."

What the fuck was going on. Black walked closer and he saw a butt naked L slightly choking Avant, who was bent over on all fours and L's stiff dick was thrashing Avant's asshole.

Black and L made eye contact and Black said, "What the fuck is going on?"

Just then, the doorbell rang and he bolted upstairs. He peeked through the blinds and he spotted two patrol cars. Two officers approached the house.

"The goddamn police. Damn. What the fuck do they want?"

KINGPIN WIFEYS II,
Part 2: The Bad Guy

Chapter 1

THE POLICEMEN'S PATROL CAR WAS FLASHING ITS LIGHTS IN THE driveway and L was raping a man in Black's basement. Black peeked through the blinds as the officers approached the house. Black thought about not opening the door, but he was sure they'd seen him drive up. Perhaps they'd followed him.

He had to calm the fuck down. There was only one patrol car and he knew that with his and L's criminal records, half the police force would be outside if they were coming for either of them. He hadn't done anything wrong. There were no drugs and he wouldn't allow them in the basement. If he didn't open the door, it would just draw their suspicion.

They rang the bell again. He recognized the two officers. They were the same two that had taken him to jail the night he'd thrown Sharee out.

One of the officers said, "Mr. Massey, how are you?"

Damn, the man remembered his name. Anytime the neighborhood police remembered your name was not a good thing, Black thought.

His partner chimed in and said, "I hope you left that crazy woman alone."

They all laughed about that night and then Black said, "How can I help you?"

"We received a call from one of your neighbors that there has been a strange car cruising the neighborhood for the past two weeks. Have you noticed anything?"

"No, I haven't noticed a thing, officer," Black lied. He was not about to help them do their job. Plus, he needed them to get the fuck out of here.

He grinned and said, "But I'll be on the lookout. If I see something, I'll be sure to call it in."

The officer passed Black a card and said, "Have a nice evening."

"Good night, Mr. Massey."

Black latched the door and bolted downstairs. L had just slipped into his boxers and was sitting on a folding metal chair, putting his socks on. Avant, still positioned on his stomach, was crying. His legs were sprawled wide and his asshole gaped open.

"We need to talk right motherfucking now."

"Can I get dressed?" L said as he laced his sneakers.

Avant glanced at Black, then at L. He wanted to die. He wished that they would just kill him. Torture was one thing but being brutally raped by a man was another. He despised Black, but he felt fortunate that Black had caught them in the act of sex. This had been the third day in a row that L had attacked him. Every night, L would come down, drag him out of the cage and lube his asshole before fucking him like a woman. L even proclaimed that he loved Avant and wanted him to reciprocate the sick love.

L followed Black to the top of the stairways. L was struggling with his zipper as he walked. "Fuck!" he yelled. L's pubic hair was pinned to his zipper. When he was done struggling with his zipper, he looked Black straight in the eyes and said, "I know what you're going to say."

"What?"

"That you ain't down with that gay shit and I understand how you feel. When I first went to prison, neither was I, but after about ten years, I broke down." L paused. "I fucked a man and my life has never been the same, and no matter how hard I struggle to fight the urge, I just can't shake it. It's like an addiction or something." He paused again and said, "You don't know the life I lived, so don't you motherfuckin' judge me. Yeah, I'm a little fucked up, but you ain't seen the shit I seen in my life."

Black wanted to say that no amount of time would make him do something that he didn't want to do. He'd known guys who'd spent decades in prison and never participated in homosexual sex, but this wasn't the time to argue with L.

"I don't care what you do. Just don't fuck Avant, man. Not in my house."

"We're in the basement."

"L, he's a man."

"A man that murdered Lani."

"You didn't know Lani."

"Who cares? Look, we've beat the shit out of him with baseball bats, fed him pet food and made him drink his own piss. And you're making a big deal out of this?"

"L, don't do it." There was no point in arguing with L. He was a savage with no comprehension. "You're getting paid to do a job. Why is it so hard not to rape this man?"

"It's not hard at all. I just want to know why?"

"Cuz I said so."

"We should just kill him then."

"We'll kill him when I say kill him."

"Why did you want Kyrie dead and not him?"

"He was an informant. The Feds would have known he was missing if we held him."

"And you don't think they know he's dead by now."

"L, just do what the fuck I say. I don't want to think about Kyrie right now."

"All right. Whatever."

Black thought back to the day at the basketball court and the two trannys that had approached the court. "So it was true what Fy-head said?"

"Why?"

"Look, man, I don't care what you do, believe it or not." Black meant that. L wasn't exactly his friend. He couldn't care less about his sexuality.

"Yeah, it was true."

"Why deny it?"

"Because I like women."

"And you like men."

"Yeah...but it didn't start out that way."

"I'm not judging you, L."

"Old habits are hard to break. I've tried."

L started to unbutton his pants and Black said, "What the fuck are you doing, man?"

"I'm going to get in the shower. If that's okay with you...boss."

Chapter 2

JADA WAS IN HER BEDROOM FOLLOWING ALONG WITH THE YOUTUBE exercise instructor on her Smart TV. Jada looked cute in her pink workout tights and sports bra. Nobody had complained about her body yet, except for the few haters that would troll her on Instagram talking about how her ass was fake, but she had to keep her body tight because there was a twenty-two-year-old girl somewhere right now trying to come for her crown and Jada wasn't ready to give it up just yet.

Jada did her lunges with five-pound dumbbells. She focused on her lower body. She would skip the arm-toning workouts. The last thing that she wanted were huge, manly looking arms or shoulders, but she could do squats and lunges all day.

Jada's phone rang, interrupting her workout. She paused the video and grabbed the phone from the bed. She didn't recognize the number. "Hello?"

"What's up, baby?"

"Who the hell is this? I ain't got time for no games. I'm in the middle of something."

"Calm down, baby. It's Fresh. Ah man, you done forgot about me already. You been cheating on me?"

"Oh, I'm sorry. I didn't know who you were and as far as cheating on you...um, maybe."

Jada had hoped that he would call, but she hadn't counted on it. Guys were so full of shit especially guys that had a little bit of money. She lay across the bed, phone still to her ear. She didn't know why, but he made her feel like a high school girl again.

"Where are you, baby?"

"In Houston, but I'll be back in Atlanta tomorrow. Can we go out?"

"I would like that." She was blushing hard as hell thinking about his beautiful hair and those long lashes. She hadn't been with a gorgeous chocolate man in forever. Damn, she missed chocolate. She said, "Baby, do you need a ride from the airport?"

"I'm getting a rental car."

"Where are you staying?"

"With you I hope."

She laughed and said, "No, that's not going to work. Not right now, but if you're good to me, I might let you stay a night or two."

"Is that right?"

"Yup."

"I think I can do that."

"That's what I want to hear."

The next day, around three, Fresh called and said his flight had made it. He'd picked up his Toyota Camry from Budget rental cars, and he was staying at the Ritz Carlton in Buckhead.

"Are we going out tonight?"

"Where do you want to go?"

"Sundial."

"What is that?"

"A restaurant. I think you'll like it."

"Whatever you say, babe."

"Okay, I'll pick you up."

Jada picked Fresh up at eight. When he got in the car, he hugged her. She smelled absolutely delicious—so delicious that he wanted to remove that little dress and eat her pussy right there on the spot.

Their reservations were for eight forty-five, so they arrived at the restaurant by eight thirty. She gave the server her name. She trailed the hostess and Fresh walked behind Jada, watching her ass bounce in her tight-ass, little black dress. His dick was throbbing as he imagined Jada on top of him riding him, her hands on his chest, gazing into his eyes. There absolutely had to be a man in her life.

The server appeared and they ordered drinks. Jada had a Lemon Drop and Fresh ordered a shot of Grey Goose.

The server brought back the drinks. He sipped his vodka and then asked, "Where is your boyfriend?"

"What boyfriend?"

He laughed and said, "Somebody is keeping your fine ass occupied."

"I have friends."

"You look like you're doing good for yourself." Fresh had noticed the designer clothes and bags as well as the fact that she drove a Benz.

"Well, my last boyfriend took good care of me."

"What happened?"

"What do you mean what happened?"

"How did he let you get away?"

"Well, he went away." Jada was silent. She sipped her Lemon Drop and stared out the window into the Atlanta night. The rain drizzling outside—the kind of weather that made her wish that she didn't have to go home alone. She wanted to cuddle.

He could tell that this was a touchy subject and he said, "You don't have to talk about it if you don't want."

She made eye contact with him and she was admiring his feminine lashes again. She had never seen a man so beautiful that wasn't gay. His strong cheekbones and that wavy hair. She just wanted to run her hands through it. Damn, he could have easily made it as a model.

He interrupted her thoughts, "Hey, did you hear me?"

"He went away."

"We don't have to talk about it if you don't want to."

"It's okay. My man is in prison. Well, he's not my man because he can't do nothing for me in there."

"That's cold."

"Wait a minute. I'll always love him. And I'll always be there for him."

"But you can't wait for him?"

"He has life."

"Damn." Fresh sipped his drink. "For what?"

"Same shit most hood dudes are into."

"Oh. Yeah."

"I think ya'll work for the same company."

"What company?" Fresh looked confused because he knew he hadn't held down a job since he was sixteen years old working at Subway, and even then, he'd quit after two weeks.

"The streets." She laughed.

"You got jokes."

"It's true."

"How do you know?"

"I can just tell. Well, for one thing you're attracted to me."

"So you've only dated D-Boys?"

"Pretty much."

"Why?"

"I don't know? We just seem to gravitate to each other."

"Is it because they have money?"

"Well, I have my own money now."

The waitress brought their food and Fresh said, "Wait a minute. Is this floor moving?"

She laughed hard as hell. "I was just wondering when you were going to figure it out."

"This is pretty cool. I was like, damn, I'm feeling this liquor fast."

"This tripped me out the first time I came too. The restaurant rotates and you can see the whole city. So, Fresh, how many baby mamas do you have?"

"I have a son."

"That's it?"

"Yup. You have kids?"

"No. Haven't been that fortunate."

"It's time for that to change. I want a daughter."

She blushed as she thought about a child with this incredible, handsome man. There was no question in her mind that she would fuck him. The question was when.

He said, "I think I had you all wrong."

She wondered what he'd meant by that.

"Look, I'm going to be honest with you. I thought you were a gold digger that just wanted some money."

"Really?"

"Yup."

She laughed and said, "So what changed that?"

"Well, you seem real open."

"Since you're a friend of Starr's friend, I trust you."

"Did you know Trey?"

"I did! But not good. I'd met him a time or two. He seemed like a good dude. He was Q's friend. They were really close which was why it surprised me that he made a play at Trey's girl. But Starr is cool, and gorgeous, so I can see why now."

"Hey, life goes on. Trey's not here."

"Life goes on. That's for damn sure."

Later that night, in front of Fresh's hotel, they sat in her car. He asked, "Are you going to valet the car and come up to the room?"

"Not tonight, babe."

"Why not? You think I'm going to judge you and that it will get back to Starr?"

"One thing about me that you'll soon learn is that I don't give a fuck about what nobody has to say about me. Nobody, including my mama."

"Well damn." He laughed. Then he leaned forward and placed his hand under her chin. She closed her eyes and he kissed her.

The next day, she invited him to her home. He used the GPS in the rental car to find out where she lived. She had cooked him baked chicken and broccoli with brown rice. Then they watched Netflix and played cards.

"Damn, you're making it hard for a man to go back to Texas. Are all ya'll Georgia girls like this?" Fresh asked.

"I can't speak for all Georgia girls." She removed the plates from the table and headed to the kitchen. He watched her ass in those tight, black yoga pants. She could feel his eyes on her so she shook her ass a little harder.

When she returned, he was standing, looking at his watch. He said, "I gotta be going."

"I want you to stay. Spend the night with me, baby."

They made eye contact and his dick came alive. He was smiling hard as hell and he said, "Hell, you don't have to ask me twice."

She laughed. "I didn't think so."

She led him into the bedroom then disappeared into the bathroom where she showered and brushed her teeth. She came back into the room wearing pink boy shorts that were lost in the crack of her ass. He was asleep when she entered the room until she nudged him.

He sat up on the bed and said, "Goddamned. What's a nigga to do with all this?"

"Oh you don't know what to do?"

"I'll figure it out."

Fresh removed his shoes and shirt, revealing a tattooed picture of a baby plastered to his chest along with the date 10-10-2011. The word Jaden was inscribed on his chest. She assumed that it was his son but she would ask about it later.

He removed his jeans and his socks until he was down to a pair of blue boxers speckled with white stars. He placed his arm around her waist and then grabbed a handful of her ass. His mouth covered her nipples and they sprang to life. She collapsed on the bed and he kissed her neck. He planted kisses all the way down to her navel. She was hoping like hell that he would yank those panties down, and seconds later he tugged at them.

He whispered, "You smell delicious. What the fuck are you wearing?"

It was just some cheap-ass lotion from Bath and Body Works, but he didn't need to know that right now. And why in the hell was he asking questions for? She needed him to place those lips on her clit and shut the fuck up.

She placed her hands over his lips and said, "Shhh."

She wanted to let his ass know that it was not okay to talk right now. His thumb clung to her lace panties, and as he struggled to yank them down, she could feel his heart pounding. Why in the hell was he so nervous? Jada was hoping this fine-ass motherfucker didn't have a small dick. Damn, that would be disappointing. She wiggled her ass a little to help him with the panties that he was struggling with. When they were down to her ankles, she flung them to the floor with her big toe. His tongue traced her belly ring then he licked her inner thighs. She was trying not to force him down, but she couldn't wait. She manhandled his head down further and when he spotted her kitty, it was delightful. Completely shaven—porn-star style. He kissed her down there and she was wishing he would hurry up and taste it or put his cock in.

Why was he taking so goddamned long? His dick had to be small. Why else would a straight man hesitate to dive into some pussy? He licked her pussy, teasing her clit with his tongue before his mouth settled on the opening. He sucked and sounded like a vacuum. Though she was enjoying this, she tightened her legs and he made his way up her body until they were face to face. She felt his rock-solid dick brush again her leg. She reached her hands down until she felt his manhood through his boxers. Long—check. Thick—check. Circumcised—check. She had been wrong. Fresh had a monster between his legs.

She whispered, "Why in the hell do you still have these shorts on?"

"I dunno. I'm a little nervous."

"No need to be nervous. Calm down. Mama is going to take care of you."

"Is that right?"

"Take 'em off. Now!"

He removed his boxers. His dick was now pointing at her, a long dark chocolate stick—a huge muscle with hundreds of veins and capillaries. It was a beautiful tool for an even more beautiful man. She shoved him back until his head rested on the pillow. She wanted him to sit back and watch her perform. She knew guys were visual and they enjoyed watching women perform oral on them. She took his dick in her mouth and stared up into his eyes. A smile was covered his face as she licked the shaft and sucked his balls. She pulled his shaft and licked it at the same time. It felt so good to him that he had to stop her.

"What's wrong?" Jada asked.

"Nothing."

"Why did you stop me?"

"I want to be inside you."

He ripped open a Gold Magnum packet. Jada wondered where it came from. Perhaps he'd had it in his hands. It was obvious that he'd come prepared for action.

She smiled and turned her ass toward him and he inserted his dick inside her as she lay on her side. He spooned her for about ten minutes before she hopped up on top of him. She could feel him deep inside her stomach. She hadn't felt like this in a very long time. He gripped her ass and it felt so damn good to her that she went into convulsions. Multiple orgasms.

Damn, she'd been wrong about him having a tiny dick. He had a monster and he knew how to use it. Hallelujah. Seconds after she came for the last time, he released inside her. She sprang from the bed and darted into the bathroom. She returned with a towel and tossed it to him.

He stood, towel in hand and made his way to the other side of the bedroom. Her eyes stayed on his dick and his ass. She noticed that he had a nice ass. She would have never imagined he had an ass like that since his clothes were never fitted.

"Can I take a shower?" Fresh asked.

"No." Then she burst out laughing. "What kind of question is that? Of course you can take a shower. What am I going to say? No."

"Hey, I don't just be assuming shit."

"I'll get you another towel and a wash cloth."

"Get a brother some lotion too. "

She disappeared and came back out with the towel, a washcloth, some soap and some watermelon lotion from Bath and Body Works.

"What the fuck is this?"

"This is what I had on."

"Oh, hell no! I ain't wearing that."

She laughed. "It was just a joke, man. I'll get you some Nivea or some coconut oil. Or maybe some Vaseline for those ashy-ass ankles."

"You got jokes."

She laughed and said, "Which one? Nivea or coconut oil?"

"Either one, I just ain't wearing that watermelon shit."

After they showered, they watched some more Netflix and then she dozed with her head lying on his chest. It was eight a.m. when her phone rang. She answered it without checking the ID.

"Jada?"

Jada was half-asleep, trying her best to focus on the name on the caller ID.

"Jada?" the voice said again.

She placed the phone to the side of her face. Still not knowing who was on the other end. She glanced at Fresh who was still asleep, lightly snoring.

The person on the other end said, "Hello?"

"Hello," Jada said.

"Jada, this is TeTe."

"Who?"

"TeTe. We met the other day. Remember you brought my car back for me?"

Of course Jada remembered her, but what the fuck did she want. Why was she calling her this early in the damned morning? They weren't friends.

Jada stood up from the bed and was about to make her way to the other bedroom, trying not to awaken Fresh, but it was too late. He stood up from the bed and she glanced at that dick. His morning erection was full and thick. She wanted to hang up on TeTe's ass and get some morning dick.

He said, "Good morning, babe." Then he headed into the bathroom to pee.

She waved and whispered, "Good morning." Then she stole a peek at his ass before she disappeared into the other bedroom.

"TeTe what can I do for you?"

"I just called to tell you that I've handled Eli's bitch ass."

"Huh?"

"I got him for what he did to me."

"What do you mean? What did he do to you?"

"He was unfaithful. Do I have to spell it out to you?"

Jada was so confused. Why did she think that she gave a fuck about her and Eli's relationship?

"Just know that he paid the price. I'll tell you when I see you again."

Jada hadn't planned on seeing TeTe again. For what? They weren't besties. Hell, they weren't even worsties. Jada sighed and thought it was too early in the morning to be listening to this.

"Do you really want to know what I did to him?"

Jada really couldn't care less, but she said, "Yeah."

"Let's just say one of his fingers is gone."

"What are you talking about?"

"I chopped his goddamned finger off."

"You're joking, right?"

"Jada, I don't lie."

"And he's still with you?"

"Hell, no! I don't give a fuck where he is. Probably back at his mama's house. I really don't know."

"You cut the man's finger off? Why did you do that?"

"Anybody that plays with my heart has to pay."

"Ok, can I call you back?" Jada said, knowing damn well that she would never call this bat-shit-crazy bitch back."

"Jada, I need a man."

Did this crazy bitch really think she was going to set her up with a man after she'd just told her she'd cut her last man's finger off?

"I just need a real man to fuck me from time to time. I don't want another serious relationship."

"I can't think of nobody off the top of my head."

"Come on, Jada. You must know plenty of men."

"You're a freakin' madam. You must know plenty of men."

"Never mix business with pleasure. I don't want a man that is or used to be a client."

"I don't know anybody."

"You think I'm crazy, don't you?"

"Why do you say that?"

"I dunno. I guess I would think I was crazy if I were you. First, I wanted to befriend the girl who my man tried to cheat with. I hid the car and made him think it was stolen. Then I tell you I cut his finger off. You can tell me, Jada. You can say I'm crazy. I've been told that plenty of times and I know I throw people off a little bit."

Jada was thinking that she needed to hang this phone up and get back to the bedroom with Fresh before he got dressed.

"It's okay. You can say I'm crazy," TeTe said again.

"Look, I don't think you're crazy. Do I think you have issues? Yes. But we all have issues."

"Ain't that the truth."

Someone was buzzing in on the other end of the phone—Black.

Jada had never been so glad to see Black's name in her life. She could now end the call with TeTe.

"Look, I'm glad you listened to me without judging me. And if you think of someone you can introduce me to, just give them my number," TeTe said.

Black hung up.

"Hey, TeTe. I gotta go. Can I call you back later?"

"Yeah."

She ended the call and called Black back, only to get his voicemail.

She made her way back into the bedroom and then slipped into the bathroom. Fresh was brushing his teeth with his finger.

"There's an extra toothbrush in the cabinet," she said.

"Thanks, babe," he said before opening the cabinet and ripping into the toothbrush packet.

She noticed that he'd gotten dressed. Damn. She had been hoping for more dick. She tugged at his belt, trying to loosen it.

He took hold of her hand. "Not right now, babe."

She made a sad face. "So, I can't get any more?"

"I gotta go, babe."

"Where you gotta go? You ain't even from Atlanta."

"I got a few friends here."

"You never told me."

"What black person in America don't know someone in Atlanta?"

She laughed and said, "I guess you're right."

"I know I am."

"Well, can I give you some head? Something to remember me by."

He smiled and said, "Maybe I can work that out."

The doorbell rang.

"You expecting someone?"

"No."

She disappeared into the living room and peeked throughout the blinds. She spotted Black's white Porsche in the driveway. What the fuck did he want?

She opened the door.

"Why ain't you pick up the phone?" Black said.

"Look, Black, you're going to have to come back."

Fresh eased up behind Jada. Black made eye contact with Fresh and said, "My bad, partner."

Jada said, "Come in, Black."

Fresh was breathing hard as hell. His nostrils were flaring.

Jada said, "This is Black. Shamari's friend."

"Whose friend?"

"My ex."

"Look, partna, I ain't trying to start shit. I was just checking up on Jada," Black said.

"For her man," Fresh said. "Look, I'm out."

"You're making a big deal out of nothing," Jada said to Fresh.

"Jada is like a sister to me, bruh, and I'm friends with her man, but Jada is her own woman. One thing about me is, I mind my motherfucking business, and what you and her got going on is between you and her."

Jada said to Fresh, "Don't go anywhere, let me speak to him for a second."

Fresh really didn't know what the fuck was going on, but Black seemed like he was cool, so he decided to stay put.

Jada stepped outside and was face to face with Black. "What the fuck is going on, man?"

"Look, I'm sorry about all this. I called first. You didn't answer so I drove over and since I saw your car, I rang the bell."

"But you saw another car. Why the fuck did you ring the bell? The extra car should have let you know that I have company."

"Yeah, but I thought it was a chick over here. Hell, it's a Toyota Camry. It never even occurred to me that you would fuck with a nigga driving a Camry."

"It's a rental car. He's not even from here."

"Look, I ain't here to judge you, and I ain't going to tell Shamari shit. He don't need to be worrying about this while trying to do his time."

"I agree. So what are you here for?"

"I'm just here to drop off some more bread for Shamari." Black peeled off a thousand dollars

"This could have waited. You know he hasn't spent the money from the last time, and you know I got money."

"I know. I was in the area and I thought about it." Black threw his hands up. "No harm, no foul."

"No problem, Black."

"Good that you've moved on. You gotta live your life. I wish I could get over Lani." Black said as if he hadn't fucked anyone since Lani's death.

"Black, would you date an older woman?"

"How old? I ain't dating no goddamned grandma."

"Mid-forties."

"Does she take care of herself?"

"Yeah and she makes her own money. Has a Jag, a Tesla and a mansion in Cobb County."

"That shit don't impress me."

"I'm just saying, she got her own money. Ain't you tired of taking care of bitches?"

"What does she do?"

"I'll let her tell you."

"What's her name?"

"Theresa, but they call her TeTe."

"TeTe? She hood?"

"Yeah, but, nigga, you hood."

"Hey, you know I don't care if she hood."

"This is her number."

"Give her mine."

"Yours change so much."

"Have her call me."

"Cool. Talk to you later." Black passed her the cash for Shamari then turned and walked back to his car.

The door to the house opened and Fresh called out, "Black!"

Black turned and faced him. "Yeah. What's up, partna?"

"What's there to do tonight?"

Damn, Jada thought. She didn't need him hanging out with Black, but what could she do to ease his suspicions.

"It's Monday. You can hit a strip club but that's pretty much it. If you're going to be around during the weekend, you can hit up Opera. That's where I go. You need somebody to hang out with, hit me up. Jada got the number.

"Okay, I'll get it from her."

Damn, Jada thought. She didn't want to give him the number. Maybe after she gave him some amazing head, he would forget about it.

But after she sucked his dick until he exploded, he cleaned himself off and asked, "What's Black's number?"

Reluctantly, she gave it to him.

Chapter 3

STARR DROPPED T.J. OFF AT SCHOOL AND THEN WENT TO HER PARENT'S house for a few minutes before arriving at Q's penthouse. She was dressed in Uggs and sweat pants with her head still wrapped. She wasn't looking her best, but hell, it was breakfast and if he couldn't accept her at her worst, he didn't need to see her at her best. He'd texted her and asked if she could stop by for breakfast. He hugged her when she walked in and led her to the dining room where breakfast was prepared—turkey sausage, grits, eggs, pancakes, Greek yogurt, orange juice and fresh melon.

"Who cooked all of this?" Starr asked.

Q laughed and said, "What do you mean, who cooked it? I did."

"Oh, I thought you had all of your meals prepared for you. You know you're Mr. Bigtime with chefs and shit."

"Oh, you got jokes. My mama did teach me how to cook, you know?"

Starr bit into a piece of melon. "Mom did a good job."

He smacked Starr on her ass and said, "Looks like your Mama did a pretty good job herself."

Starr was smiling and she said, "Damn. I'm really impressed that you cooked all of this."

"Yeah, when you said that you were going to stop by, I thought the least I could do was prepare some food."

Starr disappeared into the bathroom to wash her hands. When she reemerged, she grabbed a plate and added some turkey sausage, grits and fruit. He had some of the melon, sausage and toast on his plate.

"You're not eating grits and eggs?"

"I can't stand them."

"Are you sure you're from the South?"

"Born and raised in Houston."

"But you don't like grits?"

"Weird, I know. My brother and sister love grits and eggs, but I can't stand them."

"That is weird. What's even weirder is that you know how to cook them but don't eat them."

"Didn't have a choice. My mama showed me how to cook them and told me she didn't give a damned if I liked them or not. I had to learn to cook them for when it was my turn to cook."

Starr scooped up a spoonful of grits and tasted them. "They're good."

"You sound surprised."

"Trey never cooked for me."

"I'm not Trey."

"Definitely not. I didn't think a man could ever make me like them after Trey. But you are proving me wrong."

"I'm glad."

She kept eating her grits and savored their flavor. He stopped eating and sat watching her enjoy her food. He could watch this woman forever. He loved her and he had loved her for a while from afar.

She said, "What's wrong?"

"Nothing."

"You stopped eating."

"Just watching you."

She laughed and stopped eating her grits but still held onto her spoon. "You're making me self-conscious."

"That's a good thing. We should all be conscious of our self."

"You're right." She scooped a spoonful of yogurt.

He kept watching her and she didn't seem to be bothered by it. It was a little weird, but she felt good that he was admiring her so much. She felt special.

When she finished her grits she asked, "So what are you doing today? What are the plans?"

"Well, after you leave, I'm going to get dressed and go meet up with Fresh."

"He's still here?"

"He came back a couple of days ago, but I haven't had a chance to see him yet."

"Oh, okay. Why not?"

"He's been hanging out with your girl Jada."

"Oh really? She didn't mention that to me, but then again, I haven't had a chance to speak with her lately."

"I think he likes her."

"She's cool."

"But you said that ya'll were opposites. She don't strike me as the kind of girl that wants to settle down."

"Maybe Fresh can change that. Anyway, they're both adults. I'm sure they will sort everything out."

"Maybe."

"So you're going to meet with Fresh and then what's next?"

"Nothing much."

"So why is Fresh here so much?"

He avoided eye contact with her.

"You don't have to tell me," Starr said.

"I know what you think."

"Look, it don't matter what I think. We're not getting married."

"It does matter what you think because you matter to me."

"Then why is he here?"

"We have a big problem in Texas. I told you the cartel is holding one of my friends and they're not going to release him unless I start back working. I don't think you understand how much I meant to them."

"I have an idea."

"You have no idea."

"I guess I don't."

She finished her food and she made her way through the double doors that led into the living room. He followed her, admiring her perfect body.

Her tight outfit was like a second skin and her Uggs dragged on the floor. She was so damn feminine and he liked everything about her.

Before she could walk out the door, he said, "Hold up."

She stopped and leaned her back against the door, toying with her hair. She looked so much like a girl.

He said, "So do I get a hug before you leave?" He leaned toward her and she pushed him away.

"So I don't get a kiss?"

"You said a hug."

"I want a kiss."

"Haven't brushed my teeth and I got grits in my mouth."

"I don't give a damn. I want a kiss, woman."

"You hate grits."

"Except when they're in your mouth."

She smiled and moved toward him and they kissed.

Chapter 4

FRESH TEXTED BLACK AND THEY DECIDED TO MEET UP AT ONYX. AT eleven thirty, after six bottles of champagne and about thirty lap dances, they left and headed to the Waffle House on Piedmont. Black had his gun on him but he didn't want Fresh to get caught up in his bullshit beefs. They ordered their food. Black had biscuits and gravy while Fresh ordered the pecan waffle.

Black said, "Man, that girl Alize was really digging you."

"You think so? Her body was banging, but that face was yuck."

They both laughed.

Fresh said, "I had you all wrong, Black."

"Look, man, Jada is like a sister to me. She was one of my ex's best friends."

"What happened?"

"Murdered."

"What happened?"

"Long story but you best believe the motherfucker that did it, paid for it."

"Oh, that was the girl she and Starr were talking about."

"You know Starr too?"

"My homie is talking to her."

"Damn," Black said as he thought about Starr moving on so quickly.

"Damn, what? What do you know? You know something about Starr?"

"Starr is a good girl. I just wouldn't have thought she would have moved on so fast. Her man got murdered by his baby's mama."

"Trey?"

"You knew Trey?"

"Yeah. Trey used to come down to the H and hang out."

"Wait a minute. Are you Trey's connect?"

"I don't know nothing about that," Fresh said but Black could tell he was lying.

"Look, man, I'm not here to put your business out in the streets."

"Yeah, we used to take care of Trey."

"Well, take care of me." Black smiled.

"What?" Fresh had heard him but did he really think he was going to agree to do business with someone he barely knew? He would have to ask Jada about him.

"Look, Trey was cool, but I'm a street nigga. I'm respected all over Atlanta."

"Being known can be good and bad."

"Ain't that the truth." Black had more of the biscuits thinking to himself that he was sitting with the nigga that made Trey rich. He'd known that Trey had a great connection. A good connection is something he'd never really had, but he knew that if he could make Fresh and his homie like him, he would be set.

• • •

TeTe called Black and wanted to meet up with him. She seemed a little strange but he agreed to meet with her. They met at Club Cheetahs for lunch. She told him that she would be wearing jeans. He was sitting near the stage when she walked in, and he spotted her right away. She was damn attractive for forty-five years old he thought. She wore a pair of Paige jeans and Tory Burch ballerina shoes and had a blue Goyard bag.

Black hoped this bitch wasn't bourgeois because if she was, she was about to find out right away that he wasn't changing for nobody. She actually looked ten years younger than what she was. Her ass was a little smaller than he normally liked, but he'd decided that he would fuck her if given the opportunity.

"Call me TeTe."

"TeTe." He hugged and pulled her chair out for her.

"So you're the world famous Black."

"You've heard about me?"

She smiled revealing sparking white teeth. "Yes, you're famous."

"Really? You've heard of me?"

"Black is a common nickname."

"Yes, it is."

"And most of the Black's I know are bad."

"Not true. People just associate black with bad. Like the good guys wear white hats in cowboy movies. Black people are bad. All that shit is propaganda."

"So you're good?"

"I'll be the first to tell you I'm the bad guy."

She laughed.

"I like being bad," Black said.

"I like bad boys."

"I know."

"How do you know?"

"You wouldn't be here."

"So you like going to booty clubs in the middle of the day?"

"Is that what you think this is?"

She scanned the area. There were four girls there—all white. Only one of them had a nice booty. One girl was so damn skinny you could see her ribs showing. She was skinny as a racehorse.

"Look, I just wanted some food. When I want to see ass, I go to Onyx."

"I don't believe that."

"Why?"

"Because if you just wanted food, we would be at a restaurant and not a strip club. I think you wanted to look at some tits and ass or else we would have been at a regular restaurant."

He laughed and said, "So? I like tits and ass. Does that bother you?"

"You're not my man. Why would this bother me?"

"If I were your man, would this bother you?"

"Maybe."

The waitress appeared and Black ordered a hamburger and fries while TeTe ordered a shot of Patron.

Black said, "So, what are you looking for? You obviously don't need money."

"Is it obvious?"

"Yes. Just looking at your jewelry. You have a Goyard bag."

"How do you know handbags? I swear to god, niggas know more about women's shit than women do nowadays.

"Far from it. I've bought a few bags myself. Never a Goyard though."

"My man could have bought this one."

"I was told you don't have one."

"I don't."

"See."

"Did Jada tell you what happened to my last man?"

"No."

She laughed.

"What so funny?"

"I just thought she would have told you that's all." She paused and said, "Damn, I don't want it to be so obvious that I don't need money. Maybe I should tone it down a bit."

Black didn't want to tell her that Jada had informed him that she had her own money.

"Look, I got my own money, but what woman likes to spend her money if she don't have to?" TeTe said.

"Can I ask you a question?"

"Anything."

"What do you do?"

"I provide entertainment for men."

"Oh...you're an escort?"

"No, but I can get you one if you want."

"Damn. You're like a female pimp."

She laughed and said, "Something like that. If that's what you want to call it."

"What else would you call it?"

The waitress dropped the burger on the table and TeTe ordered another shot of Patron.

TeTe downed her Patron and said, "I don't give a damn what they call me at long as they pay me. And what do you do, Mr. Black? Your job is obviously a good one—one that allows you to go to the strip club in the middle of the day."

"Well, I own a couple of restaurants."

"Impressive."

"I think so."

"What did you do before that?"

"Dirt."

She laughed and said, "At least you're honest."

"I told you, I'm the bad guy."

"Look, I'm looking for a real man."

"A boyfriend?"

"See, that's the thing with me. If you're not boyfriend material, don't say you are because then I get expectations and with expectations come letdowns and hurt and I don't like getting hurt. If I get hurt, I gotta hurt somebody."

"Oh, I'm so scared." Black laughed.

"No, seriously. I'm not the average woman."

"I can believe that."

"Right now, I just need somebody to chill with and fuck me real good. Can you handle that?"

"What does it pay?"

"I'm not paying you."

"I was kidding. Calm down."

She smiled and said, "I knew you were."

Black ate a handful of his fries then said, "I like you."

"I think we're a lot alike."

"How?"

"I think you like to be in charge and I'm used to being in charge."

"We're both bosses."

She smiled and said, "It might not work."

"But it might." He smiled. "I think you need taming."

"And you think you can tame me...young boy?"

"I'm up for the task."

She was smiling hard as hell. She flagged the waitress down and said, "Can you bring the check?"

Black said, "Bring me the check. As long as I'm at this table, I pay. I'm the man."

She laughed and said, "Give him the check."

Black finished his hamburger, tossed a hundred dollar bill on the table and escorted her out to the valet.

The valet guy drove her white Jag to the front of the club. Black hugged her and grabbed her ass. "I can tame that ass."

She smiled and said, "I'm starting to believe you."

She peeled out of the parking lot and phoned Jada.

"Hello?" Jada's voice came through the car speakers.

"Why in the hell did you set me up with that fool? That man don't have a loyal bone in his body. Black is the kind of man that is going to cheat."

Jada was laughing her ass off. "Hey, I didn't know you were looking for a husband. I think you and Black are a lot alike."

"Maybe too much alike."

"So you don't like him?"

"As crazy as it sounds, I like him. But I know we can never be official. He is just not relationship material. But I can tell he's a lot of fun."

"Black is cool. Hey, girl, just have fun with him. You don't have to make him your husband."

"That's exactly what I was thinking. Thinking that I can have some fun with him. Maybe get some dick. He probably knows how to put it down in bed."

"I don't know cuz I've never slept with him, but he has a lot of baby mamas, so he must be doing something right."

TeTe laughed her ass off.

"Do I hear wedding bells?"

"Get serious."

"Did you really cut Eli's finger off?"

"You think I was joking?"

"Well, damn. I guess not. You cut him off? No pun intended."

"Yes, I cut his ass off. Literally."

TeTe whipped her Jag down Spring Street. She heard horns honking. Black was behind her in his Porsche. He blew kisses her way. She blushed.

"What was that?"

"Black is behind me blowing kisses."

Jada laughed. "Give it a chance."

"I can't, Jada. I can have fun. But I know myself. I will kill Black or he will kill me.

"Hey, have fun."

"That's what I intend to do. Talk to you later."

"Bye, girl."

Chapter 5

Q MET FRESH IN THE LOBBY OF THE FOUR SEASONS HOTEL. FRESH gave him a pound and said, "Damn, dawg. I been here for almost three days and this is the first time I see you?"

"I didn't know you were coming."

"I'm your little brother. I'm not some random motherfucker."

"I had some things I was doing. Business meetings. You know I'm looking into some legitimate stuff to get into around here. Besides, you were trying to get to know Jada."

Fresh smiled. "I like her."

"Seems kind of out there to me."

"She's genuine. I mean, seems like she loyal. I can deal with that. You know. Hoes will be hoes. I don't need faithfulness because I ain't going to be faithful. I need loyalty."

"How can you tell?"

"Starr said it that night we met at the cigar bar," Fresh said.

"Look, I know you don't want to talk about Jada. What's up?"

Fresh looked annoyed. "Those motherfuckers still have Rico and you act like you don't give a fuck about it."

"What do you want me to do?"

"We have to do whatever it takes to get him back. If that means we gotta get rid of the dope, then that's what we gotta do. We're talking about somebody who's like a brother to us. Somebody that's down for us."

"I know."

"His kids has been calling me every day for weeks. This thing is bigger than you. I understand that you want to stop and go legitimate and shit. But this thing is bigger than you, bruh. Way bigger than you. Marcellas, Big Country and Mann are calling every day."

Q and Fresh were suppliers to Marcellas, Big Country and Mann. Marcellas was from New Orleans, Big Country was from Memphis and Eric was from Charlotte North Carolina.

"I made all of them rich men. They should have money."

"What about me?"

"What about you?"

"I'm low on money."

Q thought Fresh had to be joking. It wasn't possible for him not to have money. Q had counted millions of dollars with Fresh. There was no way that he could be broke.

"I know you got money."

"Look, man. I'm not almost forty. I'm young, I make mistakes."

"What the hell is that supposed to mean?"

"I blow money."

"Yeah on Lean, Loud and bitches. And on that stupid-ass record label I told you not to invest in. Every motherfucker I know that put money in the music business is broke now."

"First of all, I left the Lean alone and I barely smoke. Look, it's okay for you to try to go legitimate—but not me. Yes, I made some mistakes, some young-boy mistakes, but that doesn't solve our situation."

"What are you saying?"

"Talk to Diego. Tell him that you'll take the work and then just move out of the way. I'll handle the business, so Rico can go home and everybody is happy."

"For how long?"

"How long what?"

"How long is everybody going to be happy?"

"I don't know."

"I don't want my luck to run out." Q said.

"I understand."

"I haven't slept well in a long time."

"What are you saying?"

"I don't have the balls that I used too."

To hear Q say this scared Fresh. Q had always been the voice of reason. He'd been like a big brother to him. He'd never known him to be afraid of anything. He didn't know what to make of it.

Fresh's phone rang. "Rico's son."

"His son?"

"Yeah, man. Every day he calls me asking me have I seen his Dad. But see, you don't know that because you're not there and he don't have your number, but it's bad, man, really bad."

"Damn."

Fresh made eye contact with Q and said, "Look, man, I know you don't want to do it, but let's just get Diego to send the work up this one time so he can let Rico go and then we can go on about our business."

"If we do that, he'll think that we are going to do what the fuck he says to do."

"Swallow your pride, man. He got us by the balls. It's no time to be a tough guy."

"I don't see what the big deal is. He knows that even if he only deals with you, the money is good."

"He wants you involved. He thinks you're the best businessman."

"I don't want to be involved."

"It's not what you want."

"I'll see my regulars and pass the rest off to you."

"Exactly and I was thinking of dealing with this guy, named Black, I met through Jada. Knows Atlanta and Jada says he's real."

"You trust her?."

"Look, the man already has money. I went out with him last night and everywhere I went they treated him like a celebrity. He knows Starr. Ask Starr about him."

"Hell, no. I can't ask her about this. I told you how she feels about me dealing."

"I trust him."

"Ok. Well, start off slow."

"What the fuck you think I'm going to do? Sell him a hundred kilos?" Fresh laughed.

"When are you leaving for Houston?"

"Eight in the morning."

"Okay, I'll come down this weekend and we can go talk to Diego."

Chapter 6

BLACK RECEIVED A CALL FROM A PRIVATE NUMBER. HE ANSWERED anyway. A correctional institution. He thought it was probably K.B., his friend who'd taken the rap for Chris's murder, until he heard Shamari. Shamari never called. He accepted the call.

"Yo, what's up, bruh?" Black said, glad to hear from his friend.

"Same ole, same ole. You know how it is in here."

"I know that shit too well."

"I don't have a whole lot of time to talk, but is everybody okay?"

"Everything is fine. "

"Have you seen Jada?"

"I saw her the other day."

"She hasn't answered the phone in two days."

"Do you need some money or something?" Black said, trying to get the attention off Jada. He didn't want Shamari to ask him about Jada's private life.

"Jada sent me some money today, but she won't answer the phone."

"I can go check on her if you want me too."

"I would appreciate that."

Black had been in Shamari's position before—in jail, calling to find out the whereabouts of his woman. Deep down inside he knew that Shamari knew that Jada was fucking someone else, but he wasn't going to be the one to confirm it. He knew this would destroy the man. She was his lifeblood, and he knew how much Shamari cared about Jada. That was the only thing that stopped Black from making a move on Jada. Plus the fact that she was Lani's friend.

"I'll do whatever you need me to do."

"Besides that. What else is going on, homie?"

"Not much. Laying low. You know what I mean?" There was so much Black wanted to tell him but telling Jada's business was not something he wanted to talk about, and the other things that he wanted to say, he would never speak over those recorded phone lines.

"Hey, I'm going to go. I'll hit you back later to see what you found out."

"Ok, cool. Peace, my G."

• • •

TeTe and Black were meeting at Brio's when she received a call from one of her clients. She stood and said to Black, "I'm sorry. I have to go to take care of some business."

Black looked perplexed and disappointed.

She noticed and said, "Don't worry. I'll pay for the meal."

Black was not disappointed because he had to pay for a cheap-ass dinner. He was disappointed because he had noticed her legs and the spectacular tiny black dress that clung to her body. He really wanted to see what was under there.

"What kind of man would I be if I couldn't pay for a meal?"

"Yeah, but business comes first, unless you want to pay my bills." She smiled.

"Not yet."

"Look, you can ride with me if you want. I'm just going over to the Four Seasons hotel right across the street. One of my clients is having a problem."

"I'll go with you." Black tossed two fifty dollar bills on the table and they scurried to the valets where they retrieved her Jag. They were riding, while listening to Beyoncé's "7/11" on Pandora when Black said, "So you sell pussy for real?"

"Well, not my own." She laughed. "But I've sold my own before. There have been times where I had to do what I had to do."

"You were a ho?" Black sounded surprised and very interested.

"Every woman is whether she chooses to admit it or not. You know how the game goes... bad guy." She grinned and grabbed his dick.

"You're right."

"We're all hoeing ourselves out to one thing or another."

"True. So tell me what's going on."

"Well, this one girl that I have has not been satisfying clients and she makes good money. This chick is going to make five thousand dollars for two days and she's making the man feel like he should tip her ass an extra thousand dollars. He's one of my best clients."

When they arrived at the Four Seasons hotel, TeTe and Black entered the hotel. There was a well-dressed, white businessman sitting in the lobby. TeTe approached the man, Black following closely behind. When she noticed that the man looked very uneasy with Black standing right behind her, she said, "Can I have a moment alone with him, babe?"

Black took two steps back. He still wanted to be within earshot of the conversation. This whole thing was very fascinating to him. TeTe was really pimping.

Thomas Stallings was an investment banker. He was a tall, semi-attractive man, around fifty-four years old with dark curly hair and weathered skin. He wore khaki pants and an expensive Armani shirt and driver shoes in great shape. He was one of TeTe's top clients and was not a very hard man to satisfy. Most of the time, he just wanted a hot young Asian or Latina to talk to him, but sometimes he wanted his balls licked. Nothing that TeTe figured a woman couldn't do for five thousand dollars.

Thomas Stallings was standing with his hands folded, clearly pissed off, when TeTe asked what was the problem.

"I don't like the girl."

"What don't you like about her? Her looks?"

"She's gorgeous."

"Okay. What's wrong with Nikki? She is a very beautiful girl."

"Look, I know that this is pay for play, but she's not even remotely interested in what I have to say. She's been on her phone the whole time. Texting her friends. On Facebook and not even listening to what I have to say."

"What about the sex?"

"I don't care about the sex. I'm not even in the mood for sex."

Black, an earshot away, was thinking this man had to be out of his goddamned mind. Paying ten thousand dollars for a weekend and not even thinking about fucking. He and the homies would run a train on her ass for ten stacks.

"Look, she has a bad attitude. Why can't you send Lorena?"

"She's in Dubai," TeTe said. "Look, I have the perfect girl for you." With her iPhone she presented him a picture of Tamala Wu—a half-Japanese, half-black girl.

"Is she nice?"

"The nicest."

"Sexy?"

With her thumb, she flipped to another pic. Tamala was wearing pink boy shorts, hands covering her chest. "She has small boobs," TeTe said.

"As long as they're real and she's pretty."

"Would you like to see her?"

"Yes, and could you please get the other girl to leave? I'm going to go to the bar. I don't want to see her again."

Stallings was making his way to the bar when TeTe said, "Mr. Stallings?"

He turned to face her and she passed him a hundred dollar bill. "Drinks are on me."

He examined the money, stunned that she'd offered to buy his drinks. Finally, he smiled and said, "Thank you."

"The least I could do."

Stallings continued to the bar. TeTe scanned her contacts and found Nikki's name before dialing the number. Seconds later, Nikki answered the phone. "Hello?"

"Bring your ass down here in the lobby right now."

"I'm naked."

"Put your goddamn clothes on and get your ass down here right now and bring your things. We have an unhappy client."

"Tell me what's going on."

"I'm waiting on you." TeTe terminated the call.

Black said, "You're on that pimp shit for real."

"I don't usually come to hotels, but this man has been a client for years and I trust him. Otherwise, I wouldn't be nowhere near this place."

She and Black sat in the lobby and Black was asking all kinds of questions about her business.

"So some of these guys don't even want to have sex?"

"Why is that surprising to you?"

"I mean I ain't giving nobody shit unless I'm smashing."

"That's how young boys think,"

"I'm a man."

"That thinks like a boy."

"Whatever, you say. All I know is I ain't giving no money away for nothing and obviously your client ain't either."

"I think ya'll have two different things that ya'll want to happen."

"Obviously."

Nikki Santiago exited wearing a short, backless dress, carrying a Fendi overnight bag. She was Dominican with long flowing hair, intelligent eyes and freckles sprinkled on her cheeks. Her YSL stilettos clacked as she walked toward Black and TeTe. All eyes were on her as she approached them. Black thought this bitch was fucking gorgeous as he examined her pretty, little, rhinestone-speckled toes. In addition, to think, this dude didn't even want sex from her.

TeTe stood and made eye contact with Nikki who had set her bag on the floor.

"What did he say?" Nikki asked.

"He said you weren't interested in what he had to say."

Nikki huffed and said, "That's a lie. I was listening to everything he had to say. But I will admit, listening to him talk about his son's soccer matches ain't all that important to me."

"You're getting paid well, bitch, I wouldn't give a damn if he wanted to talk about a goddamned ping-pong match, you are getting paid to listen," TeTe said.

TeTe's eyebrows raised and she took deep breaths. She had to calm the fuck down before she backhanded this thot.

"And some bitch is over in Dubai getting paid ten times as much," Nikki said.

"So, is this what this is about? You're hating on Lorena?"

"I ain't hating. I just don't see why she get all the international runs."

"Look, this man sent for her. But I ain't going to argue with your ass in here. As a matter of fact, follow me."

TeTe and Black walked toward the door. Nikki picked her bag up and followed. When they were outside, TeTe handed the valet her ticket and they all piled into the Jaguar. Nikki was crammed in the backseat, her long legs looking uncomfortable sandwiched between the seats. But TeTe didn't give a fuck about her comfort level. Nikki eyed Black, wondering who he was. She was waiting on an introduction that she wasn't going to get. She didn't need to know who the fuck Black was.

"So you're trying your best to fuck up my money because you're pissed about not going to Dubai?"

"No. I just don't want to listen to his ass cry about his kids and how bad his life is when he's a multimillionaire. I got real motherfuckin' problems."

"You know that you're not supposed to be on social media when you are with a client. I don't understand why ya'll dumb bitches gotta post every damn minute of your life on Facebook."

"I was looking at Instagram. I wasn't posting shit."

"Look, you made me loose five thousand dollars with your goddamn antics," TeTe lied. She was going to send another girl to see Thomas but Nikki didn't need to know that.

"I'm sorry."

"Sorry is not going to get my money back. But the bigger issue is you're sitting over here hating on the next bitch."

"I'm sorry."

"Like I said, sorry is not going to bring my five thousand dollars back," TeTe said then she decided to be nice to her. Play mind games. She caressed Black's legs and said, "Baby, do you mind letting your seat up for Nikki."

Black slid his seat up a little and Nikki stretched out.

Nikki said, "I'm sorry. I really am."

"It's okay. I have another client. I got somebody I want you to see later tonight. He wants a light-skinned, black girl, so you're going to have to say you're black."

"That's fine. What's it paying?"

"Same thing."

"Cool. I'll take less, since we lost money."

"Thanks," TeTe said. "Don't fuck this one up."

"I won't."

TeTe hands were on Black's thigh again and said, "Baby, let her out."

Black slid the seat up as far as he could go and Nikki exited the car. Black watching her ass swaying and as she stood in front of the valet skimming through her clutch looking for the valet ticket.

TeTe interrupted Black's thoughts. "You like that, huh?"

"She sexy but..."

"But what."

"A complete airhead."

"I don't need rocket scientists. I need thots."

"Boss lady!" Black laughed.

"You like that?"

"I love it."

Black leaned over and kissed her before they sped down Peachtree; then she pulled over in the Phipps Plaza parking lot and sucked his dick until he came.

Chapter 7

TEN O'CLOCK THE NEXT MORNING, BLACK SHOWED UP AT JADA'S house without calling and she wasn't too happy when she opened the door. She opened the door wearing a purple doo-rag and a house robe.

"Black, what the fuck do you want? Why do you keep showing up at my house unannounced like I'm your woman?"

"It's 'Mari"

"What about Mari?" Jada said. Had something happened to Shamari? Her heart raced. God don't let him be delivering some bad news about Shamari.

There was a long pause and Jada demanded, "What the fuck happened to Shamari?"

"Nothing happened. He called me yesterday. I think he knows you have somebody."

"First of all, I don't have nobody. So I fucked somebody, big deal."

"Can I come in?"

She stepped aside and he entered her home and took a seat on the armchair. She sat on the sofa. She was self-conscious about her morning breath. She opened the Chanel clutch bag that was lying on the coffee table and got a pack of gum out. She offered Black some but he declined. She then popped a piece in her mouth.

"Look, he made me promise to check on you."

"Okay, you knew I was fine."

"And I told him. He said that he's been calling you and you haven't answered."

"Look, I spoke to him last night."

"Okay, cool. Look, I'm just doing what he told me to do. Just so you know, Jada. I haven't been running my mouth about you and Fresh."

"Black, Shamari has life. What the fuck am I supposed to do? Stop living?"

Black knew that a girl like Jada was not going to stop living. She was going to have fun and see men. Hell, she was doing that even when Shamari was out.

"You trying to make me feel guilty?" she asked.

"Not at all."

"Why are you here and why so early in the fucking morning?"

"Shamari told me to check. That's all."

"You know my number."

"He said he couldn't reach you."

"I talked to him last night. I told you. Hell, I don't answer my phone every time he calls."

"You know how dudes in prison are."

"I'm not the one locked up, he is."

Black stood and said, "Hey, I did what I told him I was going to do." He was about to make his way to the door when he said, "Jada, I need a favor."

"I already told you. I ain't making no drug run for you."

"Not that."

"What?"

"Talk to Fresh about me. Tell him I'm good people."

"What the fuck are you talking about?"

"Look, I need a plug. A connect."

Jada stood and said, "I ain't about to get myself involved in that shit."

"Come on, Jada."

"I gave you Shamari's plug."

"I don't want to go to Cali. It's too damn far. Plus, I hate meeting new people and since I met Fresh, I think he's good people."

Jada was ushering Black toward the door. "Look, Black, I'm going back to sleep."

Black stopped and said, "Oh, I went out with TeTe last night."

Jada laughed.

"Why are you laughing?"

"What did you think of her?"

"She's a boss. Cool as hell."

"You think so?" Jada said thinking about TeTe telling her that she cut Eli's finger off, but Black didn't need to know what.

"You know something I don't know?"

"Look, she's cool. I just met her a few weeks ago."

"Yeah, I had a good time."

"Good." She pushed Black toward the door.

Black said, "Jada, will you think about what I said?"

"Look, I ain't getting myself involved in no drug conspiracy, Black. You need to get somewhere and sit your ass down."

She wanted to ask him about Avant but she knew, with him, there were some things that she was better off not knowing.

• • •

Later that night Fresh called Jada and she asked him to meet her at the Woodfire Grill. They met up a couple of hours later.

The waiter came up to the table and said, "What would you like to have?"

"Water with lemon," Jada said.

Fresh ordered a chef's salad.

Jada said, "So, what did you want to talk to me about that we couldn't talk about over the phone?"

"Black."

"What about him?"

"Is he cool?"

"Yeah."

"I mean is he sheisty?" He dug into his salad, plucking out a pepperoncini. He searched her eyes for the truth.

Jada thought to herself, why was Fresh staring at her eyes so hard? His eyes were so intense that they penetrated her soul. Those long feminine lashes looking incredibly beautiful to her. She turned from his gaze.

"What do you know about him?" Fresh asked.

"I think it's a bad idea."

"I'm listening."

"Look, trouble finds Black. He's always in some bullshit. He has money and he plays by the rules as far as the money is concerned."

Fresh dropped his fork and picked up a packet of Ranch dressing. He squeezed every drop of dressing out of the packet.

"What don't you like about him, babe?"

She stared at him with concern on her face "He has enemies."

"Ok. I have enemies. We all have enemies."

"People want him dead."

"Tell me about him."

"Black had this guy named Chris killed and Chris's brother and his friend are after him."

"Who else?"

"Well, this nigga named Shakur is after him because he thinks that Black killed our friend Lani."

"Did he?"

"No, but a lot of people believe that she would still be here if it wasn't for Black. And a lot of people think he had something to do with it." She paused and guzzled her water. "But I don't think so."

"Why?"

"He loved Lani."

"Okay a couple of niggas want to kill him, as with most hustlers. What I'm interested in is, does he owe anybody money or is he a rat?"

"No to both of those questions."

"Okay."

"But I don't think you should deal with Black. He's bad news, I'm telling you."

"I'm a grown man."

Jada threw her hands up and said, "Okay."

Chapter 8

FRESH AND Q MET UP WITH DIEGO AT THE RESTAURANT AGAIN. Diego's sister poured each man a glass of water and Q was pissed that he had to be back in Houston. He'd rather be in Atlanta with Starr, cooking her breakfast or dining on the roof overlooking the Atlanta skyline. When Anna poured his glass, Q made sure he stared at her ass because he knew this would piss Diego off. He couldn't care less about pissing Diego off.

Diego sat across from Q, watching his eyes follow his sister's ass and finally he said, "Aye, motherfucker. I'm over here."

"I know." He smiled.

"You need to be concerned about your friend instead of watching my sister. As a matter of fact, get the hell out of here, Anna."

"Dude, don't flatter yourself. Your sister is average, at best."

"But you were looking at her."

"Maybe."

Diego smiled and said, "I want to make peace with you, and if you want to fuck my sister, I can arrange that. I need you. Well, we need each other."

"Let Rico go."

"Rico is fine."

"I didn't ask you that."

"But I told you."

"Where is he?"

"Mexico."

"What the fuck is he doing in Mexico?"

"He's fine. He's getting a big bowl of beans and a glass of water. Trust me, he's okay."

"Why would I trust you?" Q said.

Fresh said, "We're going to do whatever you need us to do to let Rico go."

"You know what you need to do." Diego said.

Q said, "We're going to do it."

"Do what?"

"Get rid of the thousand kilos."

Diego said, "I'm going to need you to get rid of two thousand kilos."

"What?"

"Two thousand or no deal."

"You're out of your mind."

"Rico is."

"Let me see him."

"He's in Mexico."

"Take me to Mexico."

Fresh looked at Q and whispered, "Are you out of your mind?"

Q pulled Fresh aside and said, "Nothing is going to happen to us. He needs us."

"I ain't going to Mexico. He needs you, not me. He's said that already."

"I'm going."

"I'm not going. You go by yourself."

"Shut the fuck up then."

Q and Fresh approached Diego. "We wanna go see him tomorrow."

"Look, you're going to profit close to four million dollars and you're going to get your friend back. That, my friend, is a win-win for you."

Q stood up and made his way out of the room. Fresh followed him through some double doors out to the dining room area. When they were outside, Q heard someone call his name. When Q turned, he recognized the man immediately. Gordo was a short man with a round baby face and a crew cut. At first glance, Gordo could be mistaken for a white man, but he was one hundred percent Mexican. Gordo and Diego were first cousins. Two brother's sons. Both of their dads had been murdered during cartel violence when they were younger, and their uncle Ramon was a cartel leader. He was both Gordo and Diego's connection, but unlike Diego, Gordo was fairly rational.

"Gordo."

Gordo followed Q and Fresh out to Q's car and said, "I heard about what happened. I'll do whatever I got to do to make sure your friend is safe."

"I really do appreciate it, man. I'm going to Mexico to see him tomorrow."

"I'll go with you if you want me too," Gordo said. He knew Q wasn't too fond of Diego and he knew that Q would be at ease as long as he was there.

"I would appreciate it if you did."

"You know, my cousin have...what you call..." Gordo was looking in the air trying to find the right word in English. "...Complejo."

"Yeah, he has a complex."

"He wants everybody to know he is boss."

"I don't give a fuck about him."

"I will tell him that you will travel with me."

"This will piss him off."

Gordo laughed and said, "I don't care about he."

Gordo's English was pretty good but every now and then, he said the wrong word.

"Thanks, Gordo."

"Take my number. When this blow over, I want to work with you."

"Look, Gordo, I don't want to work."

"You work when you want to work with Gordo. I don't force you do nothin', my friend."

"I'm not staying in this business."

"Take number anyway. Call me. I will meet you tomorrow and we head to Juarez."

Q punched Gordo's number in his phone. "Thanks, Gordo." Q fired up the Ford Fusion rental and they bolted away.

The next day, Gordo, Q and Fresh crossed the Mexican border. There was a driver waiting for them in a black SUV. Gordo ordered the man to drive them straight to his Uncle Ramon's compound. Q had been there a few times but this was Fresh's first time in this part of Mexico. The streets were littered with trash and poor people and children were standing outside begging for money. Fresh thought that even though it was rough in certain parts of Houston, this was ridiculous. A man jumped in front of the SUV. The driver barely missed the man.

The driver lowered the window and said, "Get the fuck out the way!" He said in Spanish.

The man said, "Please, please. My wife and children have not eaten in days."

Q and Fresh observed the family of four standing on the side of the road. The little boy was barefoot and wrapped in a blanket. The little girl had matted hair and clung to a doll that had to be at least three years old. The man's frail wife certainly looked like she hadn't eaten in days.

The driver was about to speed off when Gordo said, "Stop."

The driver halted and Gordo threw three gold coins out the window.

The man said, "Gracias, senor."

He then scooped the coins up quickly before anybody could see him. He knew the worth of those coins. If anyone saw the coins, they would surely get him and his whole family assassinated. The driver sped off.

Gordo and Diego's Uncle Ramon hadn't been to the compound for the past two weeks. He was on a business trip in the southern part of Mexico. The compound included brick walls and was gated like a prison. There were three stucco buildings with the main building in the center. Two armed men carrying assault rifles stood at the guard station. The driver stopped them at the entrance, but when the men at the station spotted Gordo, they opened the gate. When the SUVdrove up to the main building, Q and Fresh spotted Diego and a group of men playing soccer. The men were dressed in Chinos and wife-beaters. Tats covered their arms and faces. The game stopped when the door opened. Q and Fresh approached Diego.

Q said, "I want to see Rico."

"Carlos, take them to the prisoner," Diego said.

"Carlos was a smallish, compact man with a crew cut, an oval face and a very scraggly Mexican handlebar mustache. He led Q, Gordo and Fresh into a wing of the main building. Rico's room was at the end of the hall. Carlos inserted the metal key in the keyhole and opened the huge steel door. The sunlight burst into the room. Rico was curled up on the floor, butt naked, wearing only a single gold chain with a locket which held a baby picture of his daughter Ivy, who was eighteen now. He screamed when the light smacked him in the face.

"Please don't beat me! Please don't beat me!" Rico cried.

Fresh said, "What the fuck? What the fuck? Man, this room is smaller than my goddamned closet"

Gordo conversed with Carlos in Spanish. "Get him some goddamned clothes."

Carlos said, "Diego will be upset."

"Fuck Diego."

Q kneeled down to Rico, who was clearly a broken man. "Rico? Rico? It's me, Q."

Rico opened his eyes, trying to focus on Q. They made eye contact before Rico said, "Get away from me. Get away from me. Please, get away from me." He scooted to the corner of a room with his hands shielding his face.

Q kneeled beside his friend who hadn't showered in weeks. His body odor was overpowering. Q took hold of Rico's arms and Rico took a swipe at Q barely missing his chin. "Don't bother me, motherfucker." Saliva was rolling down the side of his mouth.

"Rico, it's me. It's me, Q. I came to take you with me."

Rico and Q locked eyes. Q ran his fingers through Rico's afro and said, "It's me, Q."

Rico grinned. He recognized Q but he was a broken man. His hair hadn't been cut in weeks and there was a patch of grey hair in the center of his afro.

Q said, "I've come to get you. Don't worry. You're going to go with me."

Rico shook his head without responding. Carlos came running back with a pair of jeans and a flannel shirt. He passed them to Q and then he and Fresh stood Rico up.

They clothed Rico and when they were done, Q whispered, "I love you, champ."

There was no response from Rico. The man was on the verge of losing his mind. Rico sat down on the floor Indian style. Carlos was about to close the door of the room when Rico looked at Fresh and Q.

"Don't leave me," Rico said.

The door slammed shut and Rico's face disappeared. The men headed out to the yard where the men had resumed their soccer game. Q approached Diego and snatched him up by the collar.

"Motherfucker, I will kill you if anything happens to him."

The soccer game stopped and suddenly Q had seventeen assault rifles pointing at him.

Diego said, "Let me go or you won't make it out of here."

Gordo wedged himself between Q and Diego and ordered the men to lower their weapons. They all did because they knew that if Gordo were ever harmed, his uncle would have all of them murdered.

Gordo said to Q, "You trying to get killed? I need you and Fresh to walk in front of me."

They walked to the front of the compound where the driver awaited them and drove them back to the border.

Chapter 9

JADA WAS DRESSED VERY CASUALLY IN RIPPED, FADED SKINNY JEANS, a turtleneck and a pair of Uggs. Her hair was up in a bun. She stepped into the elevator, pressed P, and was on her way to Big Papa's penthouse. She had a cup of coffee from Starbucks in her hand and as soon as she exited the elevator, she saw grinning-ass Big Papa standing there, looking at her like she was ice cream and cake.

She hugged him and said, "Hey, Boo."

She was so phony to him but he was so dumb that he would never pick up that she didn't give a damn about his fat ass.

"Damn, baby. You're smelling good. What are you wearing?"

"I can't tell you that. You think I'm going to tell you so you can go buy it for some of your other hoes?"

He chuckled as if his big ass really had a lot of hoes.

"Come on, you gotta tell me what that is. You're driving me crazy."

"That's my job."

She trailed him into the living room, watching his underwear struggle to cover his ass crack. Yuck. He sat on a sectional, and she sat on a yellow armchair across from him. He still had a stupid-ass grin on his face. Nappy whiskers covered his pudgy face.

"Why are you smiling so hard?"

"Glad to see you, that's all."

"Would you quit it? It's freaking me out."

"Damn, a brother can't be happy to see you?"

"Yes, but you just saw me a week ago."
"I like you, Jada."
"I know you do."
"You don't like me?"
"I do like you Big—I mean Ty."
"You can call me Big Papa, since I know now that's what you were calling me behind my back." He laughed.
She laughed too and sipped her coffee.
"So what brings you here, Jada?"
"Wanted to talk."
"About?"
"Shakur."
"Shakur? What about him?"
"Look, Shakur was after Black and I was just wondering since Lani was murdered, has he let that go?"
"As far as I know. I mean I don't talk to him every day."
"Call him."
Papa stood and wobbled his way into the bedroom before returning with his iPhone. He dialed Shakur's number. He activated his speaker.
"Yo, what's up, big guy?"
"What's up, bruh? I'm over here with Jada."
"Tell her I said hey."
"She heard you. You're on speaker."
"Oh, I'm on speaker?"
"Yeah, you want me to take you off?"
"No, it's all right."
"Hey, Shakur," Jada said.
"She wants to ask you something," Big Papa said.
He passed her the phone. There was saliva on the phone and it smelled like shit. She held it away from her mouth. "Shakur, can you come over? I want to talk to you."
"Give me thirty minutes."
"Cool." She ended the call. Big Papa sat beside her on the sofa. She felt uncomfortable with him beside her and all she could think about was that his breath usually smelled like hot shit.
He glanced at her handbag and said, "Is that the bag that I bought you?"
"Yes, Daddy, it's one of the bags that you bought me. You've been so good to me, I've lost track of the bags that you've gotten me."
"I try my best."
"You're very good to me," Jada said. She knew where he was going. Over the last month or so, he'd been trying to get in her panties and she had denied him. She was sure that it was just a matter of time before he cut her off. She would be fine with that because there was no way in hell she was going to fuck his fat ass.
Big Papa extended his arms and tried to hug her. She shoved him away

and he made a sad face. "What's wrong, baby?"

"Shakur is on the way and I don't want to get all horny with him on the way," she lied.

"I just think you don't like me touching you."

She wanted to say, hell, no I don't want your fat, disgusting ass touching me but instead she smiled and said, "That's not it, Daddy."

"What is it then?"

"I'm not in the mood."

"Cycle again?"

"No." She knew she couldn't use that excuse. She'd used that excuse a few times and one time he'd even gone down on her anyway.

"What is it?"

"Look, I didn't come over here for this. I came over here to make sure this beef was squashed between Shakur and Black."

"Why do you care?"

"I don't want anybody to get hurt."

He placed his hand on her leg, which was partially exposed through the ripped jeans. "I've always thought ripped jeans were sexy as hell."

"Really?" She wanted to move his hand but she thought maybe if she left it there, he wouldn't press her for sex.

"Can I get a kiss?"

"No."

"Why not?"

"Why are you asking for a kiss? Most men just take it. You have to be bold. A planned kiss is never sexy. Remember that."

"So if I kissed you out of the blue, you wouldn't be mad?"

"If the mood was right, and you stole a kiss, that would be so fucking hot."

She couldn't imagine him slobbering on her, trying to kiss her. All she could think about was that stinking-ass phone and the germs that had accumulated on it. Jada didn't want to continue with Big Papa. He was a nice guy, and he didn't deserve to keep getting used by her.

Big Papa's cell phone rang. It was the front desk. Shakur was in the lobby. Papa ordered security to send him up, and a few moments later, Shakur was standing in the living room. He was wearing a skintight, black nylon Under Armor shirt and his six pack was imprinted though the tight shirt. His locks were pulled back and bound with a rubber band. The man's body was like a superhero or something out of a movie. Jada would have fucked him right then and there if she didn't feel it would dishonor Lani. Besides, she was there for conversation only. Shakur hugged Jada and then took a seat on the sectional opposite Big Papa.

Jada said, "How you been?"

"Doing good. Just working out, trying to keep my mind off Lani."

"Yeah, it's tough for all of us."

Shakur's eyes became misty and said, "I don't think you understand. This is the first woman that I actually gave a damn about. I can't help but think about what could have been."

Jada felt very bad for Shakur. She could tell he was very sincere.

Big Papa laughed and said, "Got my dawg getting all soft and shit."

"I loved her," he said then he stood and made his way to the bathroom. Jada stared at his ass as he made his way to the bathroom. For a brief moment, she wondered what it would be like to fuck Shakur and Fresh at the same damn time. She could deep throat Fresh while Shakur fucked her in the ass.

Shakur reappeared and took his position back on the sofa.

Jada said, "I just want to know if the beef is over between you and Black."

"Did Black send you over here?"

"No, he didn't."

"Why are you asking that?"

"Lani is dead, Shakur. There is no reason to beef, right?"

"Except the fact that I just don't like that punk motherfucker."

"So let me get this straight," Jada said. "You don't like that punk motherfucker, so that's a reason to beef with him?"

"Look, I don't give a fuck what anybody say. He had something to do with Lani's murder."

Jada didn't want to tell Shakur what she knew about Kyrie killing Lani because that would only reaffirm what Shakur already thought—-that Black had something to do with the murder.

"So this is worth somebody possibly getting killed? You can't bring Lani back, Shakur. She's gone."

"I know she's gone and I can't bring her back, but I can take the motherfucker out that killed her."

"Please, Shakur, let it go. I've seen too much bad shit happen. I don't know you, but I know you're a close friend of Ty's and I don't want nothing to happen—-"

"Happen to who? Not me. You need to go talk to Black and say a prayer over his ass."

Jada could see this was going nowhere, and there was no use in trying to persuade him to let the beef go. Jada stood and hugged Big Papa and then shook Shakur's hand. She let herself out of the penthouse.

Chapter 10

ELI HAD COME BY TO GET HIS THINGS AND EVEN THOUGH TETE HAD chopped his finger off, he still wanted to be with her. He didn't want to give up his life of luxury. But despite his pleas, she'd told him to get the fuck out. She liked Eli, but there was no doubt in her mind that she would kill him if he ever fucked around on her again. So to avoid all that, she sent him on his way, and it was a win-win for everybody. Eli got to keep his life, and she was single to do whatever the fuck she wanted and right now, she was trying to see what this Black character was all about.

She was lying on her bed finishing up an episode of the Real Housewives of Atlanta when she texted Black: *I wanna see you. Can I take you to dinner?*

Black: *What time.*

TeTe: *8:30. Where do you wanna go?*

Black: *Spoondivits? I don't know. You tell me.*

TeTe: *Definitely not Spoondivits. What about Oceanaire?*

Black: *Never been there but since you're paying. :-)*

TeTe: *So you wanna come pick me up?*

Black: *Where did you say you lived again?*

TeTe: *I never said, but I live in Cobb.*

Black: *So do I.*

TeTe: *Perfect, see you soon.*

Black: *:-)*

Black drove up to TeTe's huge cobblestone home with the wrap around driveway. He spotted the white Jaguar. He said to himself. "This bitch got it going the fuck on."

He dialed her up and she answered. "I think I'm outside," Black said.

She peeked outside. "I'm still getting ready, come inside."

Black made sure his gun was tucked under the armrest and he had a couple of ounces of Kush in a small jar that he put away as well. He sprayed the car with Febreze just to make sure the scent didn't linger.

Seconds later, she stood at the door wearing a black dress that clung to her body. Her tiny-ass waist made Black want to wrap his arms around her and that's exactly what he did as soon as he approached her. He gripped a handful of her ass and held it for a long time.

He noticed she was wearing vanilla and said, "You smell so goddamned delicious. Smelling like a nana pudding in this motherfucker. Making me wanna eat yo ass up."

"Don't say something you ain't prepared to do."

"Don't call me out."

She laughed and said, "I'm calling you out."

"No, we gotta go. I have something I gotta do later on."

"More important than getting some pussy?"

"We're going to get to that."

"We are?"

She turned so her back was facing him. "Zip me up."

Black's big-ape ass hands struggled with the delicate-ass zipper. He was careful not to break the zipper. Finally, he got it up.

"Mommy, Mommy," a voice yelled. Black glanced up the spiral staircase and there was a pretty, little girl with pigtails.

TeTe said, "That's my daughter, Butterfly." Then she waved her downstairs and said. "Come downstairs and say hey to Mr. Black."

Butterfly made her way down the spiral staircase playing with her iPhone.

Black said, "Hey, Butterfly." He kneeled then dug into his pocket and handed her a hundred dollar bill.

TeTe said, "What do you say, Butterfly?"

Butterfly smiled and said, "Can I have another one?"

Black laughed his ass off and said, "You got game."

TeTe said, "Don't give her little ass shit. What do you say?"

Butterfly poked her lip out and said, "Thank you."

Black passed her another hundred dollar bill against TeTe's will.

Black said, "I have a daughter about your age. Maybe one day ya'll can play together."

Butterfly said, "What's her name?"

"Tierany."

"That's a pretty name."

"TeTe said, "Go to your room. Mommy is going out for dinner."

Butterfly lips were poked out again as she trotted away.

"You leaving her here by herself?"

"No. Her nanny is here."

Black led TeTe to his Porsche and being the complete gentleman, he opened the door for her. When he fired up the Porsche, "No Type" by Rae Sremmured blared through the speakers. When he saw her displeasure, he switched the music to Tinashe's "Pretend" and they sped off.

"I like hip hop too, you know?"

"What do you like, OG?"

She laughed and said, "Biggie."

"Biggie? Biggie aight, but that's so old school."

"That's what I like. I like when they were actually saying something. But I do like some of Lil Wayne's and Drake's stuff."

"Old school, you be up on shit."

"Young boy, I'm going to teach yo ass a lesson."

"I want you to take advantage of me."

They both laughed and sped through the suburban neighborhood. Black hopped onto the Interstate and headed downtown. Black exited onto Lennox road Northeast ,when a forest-green Jeep Cherokee pulled alongside them, lowering their window. TeTe spotted them first as the men in the jeep tried to get her attention, requesting her to lower her window.

She nudged Black and said, "Baby, I think these guys want directions." She lowered her window.

Black unbuckled his seat belt and shoved her to the floor. Then he pressed the gas pedal to the floor.

"Get down!" he yelled.

That's when the men opened fire. Black shot across the median and barely escaped an oncoming car. The Porsche skidded for about twenty yards before flipping over on the side. The passenger window shattered and the airbags exploded in their faces. TeTe's leg slammed hard against the dash.

Black said, "You okay, baby?"

TeTe said, "What the fuck was that about?" She hobbled out of the car, but she was fine other than her knee and her heart being about to jump out of her chest. Black's door was stuck and his leg was broken. She tried to help him out but he couldn't move his legs and he was too heavy for her to move.

Chapter 11

NOBODY KNEW WHERE THE HERO HAD COME FROM, BUT HIS BLACK F15 pickup truck was in the median of the road. The hero was six foot four with dirty blond hair and weighed about two hundred and forty pounds. He wore a red flannel shirt, jeans, boots, and a John Deer ball cap. He looked like he had leaped off the pages of an L.L. Bean Catalog and was certainly big enough to drag Black out of the car. The hero ordered Black to turn his head to avoid the glass and he kicked in the windows. Then dragged Black from the car.

Black was still fully conscious and he thanked the hero. But there was a matter of two ounces of OG Kush and the gun in the glove compartment. He knew that the police were coming and if they got their hands on that gun, he would be fucked and there would be no way around it. He was a convicted felon and there was no way he could get out of it. Black called TeTe. She kneeled down with the hero standing over them, wanting to know if he could be of any further assistance.

Black whispered. "I need you to get the gun out of the car. It's in the glove compartment."

The hero heard the last part of the sentence. "You need me to get something from the glove compartment? I'll get it."

Black said to the man, "My leg's in pain. Can you bring me something to elevate it?"

The man dashed to his truck and got a crate that was in the cab.

Black was thankful for the man's help, but there was no doubt in this mind, that this great blue-blooded, American hero would let the cops know about the marijuana. TeTe retrieved the gun and the weed. She dumped the weed into a nearby trashcan and placed the gun in her purse. Then they waited there until the ambulance came.

The police and firemen came and the police questioned TeTe about what happened. She simply stated the obvious. She didn't want to talk to them, but what was she going to say. She didn't know what happened, but she was in the car, so she knew that they wouldn't buy that for one moment. She told the officer that two men pulled alongside them and opened fire.

"Can you give a description?"

"I can't. It happened so fast."

The officer said, "There is one witness saying that it was a forest-green Jeep Cherokee. Does that sound about right?"

"Yes," she agreed.

Black was being attended to by the paramedics when the police came up to him. "Could you tell us what happened, sir?"

Black said, "I have nothing to say."

The officer said, "Do you want to talk later?"

"No."

They loaded Black into the ambulance. TeTe climbed in with them and rode with Black to the hospital.

• • •

Black was in Emory University Hospital in room 664.

The doctors had to place a rod in Black's leg. His fibula had been shattered. Ironically, it was the same one that had fractured before when Chris had riddled his car with bullets. He knew that his leg would never be the same, but he was grateful that he was still alive. He was resting up in the hospital after his surgery when came in. She spotted an old lady by his side with a big old Bible in her lap .She figured the woman had to be Black's grandmother. She kind of reminded her of her own grandmother, Big Ma. Black smiled when he saw her enter the room.

The old lady turned and said, "I'm Nana. I don't believe that we've met."

"I'm Theresa." TeTe extended her hands.

Black said, "You're looking at the woman that raised me, baby."

"I didn't do a good job obviously."

Black laughed and said, "Ha, Ha. Very funny."

TeTe sat on the chair beside Nana and Black said, "Nana, can I talk to Theresa for a moment?"

"Yeah, go ahead." Nana said as she sat there with her Bible in her lap.

"Alone, Nana."

Nana made her way to the entrance. "I'll go down to the vending machines."

When the door closed, Black said, "I didn't tell Nana what happened, so don't mention it."

"Why is she here then? I know she's your grandma, but if you didn't want her to know, why did you call her?"

"The hospital wanted me to call somebody before I went into surgery."

"And you called her?"

"Nana's number was the only number I could remember. She still has a house phone and the number has been the same since I was eight years old."

She stood over him, looking down at him. He looked weak in his hospital gown and his leg propped up. She stole a glance at his dick. It wasn't erect but still very impressive.

"Are you okay?" she asked.

"I'm fine."

"You wanna tell me what was that all about?"

"I don't know."

"Look, that shit wasn't random. Somebody wants you dead and I need to know if I'm going to keep fucking with you."

Black was thinking to himself that this bitch had to be crazy to deal with somebody like him. Why would she want to be involved with him? She'd just been shot at.

"It's a long story."

"I got time."

"Not with Nana here."

"Tell me what happened." He could tell that she was growing impatient. He thought that he owed her that much. She was in the car with him and she didn't run away.

"My ex-girlfriend Lani—"

Nana barged into the room and said, "I'm going to leave."

TeTe said, "That's okay, Nana. You can stay. I'm going to leave and I'll come back later." She kissed Black on his forehead and said, "Mister, we need to finish this conversation as soon as you get out of the hospital. Please call me."

"I will."

TeTe hugged Nana and said, "It was a pleasure meeting you."

"Same here."

Chapter 12

TWO DAYS LATER, BLACK GOT OF THE HOSPITAL. SINCE THE PORSCHE was totaled, he was forced to drive the Camaro that he'd given to Asia, his baby mama. Since she hardly drove it, she said it would be okay if he kept it. It was ten in the morning when he drove to Jada's place.

She answered the door and said, "Black, what the fuck have I told you about popping up at my house?" Then she noticed the crutches and the Aircast. "What the fuck happened to you?"

"Can I come in?" He hobbled inside and Jada led him to the kitchen. They sat at the bar and she offered him some water.

"You got anything stronger?"

"Yeah, what do you want?"

"Patron."

"It's ten in the morning."

"I don't care."

Jada made her way to the liquor cabinet. Black couldn't help but notice her Victoria Secret shorts crawling up her ass. She poured him a glass of Patron and herself one as well.

He laughed and said, "I thought it was too early to drink."

"I got a feeling what you're about to tell me requires a drink."

"Yeah, I lost my phone. Well, I think it's in my car. My car that looks like a sardine can now. So I have a new phone and I didn't have your number. That's why I popped up."

Jada passed him the drink and then took a swig of her own. He downed his drink right away and she poured him another. He was watching that fantastic ass the whole time. He knew he would never fuck her but there was no harm in dreaming.

She passed him the second glass of Patron and placed the bottle in front of him.

"Someone pulled up alongside me and TeTe and opened up the other night."

"Oh my God. Is she okay?"

"She's fine. I'm the only one that got hurt and I'm fine. I just broke my leg, but other than that, I'm okay."

"I swear, boy, you got nine fucking lives."

"I do, don't I?" He laughed.

"That shit ain't funny. You are blessed, but I'm afraid one of these days it's going to catch up with you."

"Surely hope not. But I know if it does, I've done a lot of fucked-up shit.

"Are you saying you'll get what you deserve?"

"I ain't saying all that."

"How long do you think you're going to keep getting away with shit, Black?"

"Look, that's why I'm here."

"You want a prayer?"

"Do you know where Shakur lives?"

"No."

"If you did, would you tell me?"

"No. Look, Black, how do you know Shakur had something to do with this? It could have been Chris's brother. You don't know who it was."

"You right. I don't know. But I need to find out."

"Look, I ain't getting in the middle of it."

Black could tell that Jada meant what she said. "You talk to Mari?"

"He just called. I'm going to see him tomorrow."

Black heard what Jada said, but he wasn't listening. His mind was on Shakur. He had thought for sure that Jada would give him some information on his whereabouts.

Black stood and hobbled through the kitchen. Jada trailed behind and Black stopped at the front door. "I almost forgot, have you spoken with Fresh?"

"Yes, last night."

"Can I have his number?"

Jada disappeared into her bedroom. Those tight shorts barely containing that big, bouncing ass. Of course, Black stole a peek but he had more important things to worry about. He knew that he needed to find out who in the hell was trying to kill him and he knew where to start. He would have to go in the hood and find out who knew Shakur. He would ask other D-Boys and strippers. Strippers knew everything about everybody.

Jada came running back with her phone in her hand and she mouthed off Fresh's phone number.

Black saved the digits in his new phone.

• • •

Later that night, Black met TeTe at Bistro Nikkos, an elegant little French restaurant that had expansive ceilings and artwork from Paris. It was one of TeTe's favorite restaurants. It was very classy but affordably priced. TeTe was dressed in a white pantsuit and flats. She was carrying a YSL clutch. Black was dressed in jeans and Louis sneakers, his usual Dope-Boy apparel, and an Aircast on his leg.

When he entered the restaurant, TeTe waved him over to the booth where she was seated. When she saw him struggling to get inside the booth, she said, "I'm sorry, I should have gotten a table."

"It's okay. I'd rather sit in a booth." He managed to get his feet planted under the table.

He stared at her for a while and she looked absolutely amazing. Sometimes he'd forget that she was in her forties. He skin looked exceptional tonight. Black gazed around and saw that everybody including TeTe was dressed very well and he said. "Damn, babe. Why didn't you tell me that I should dress up?"

"If I did tell you, would you have dressed up?"

"No."

"Exactly why I didn't tell you."

"So you on your bourgeois shit tonight?"

"Not at all." She sipped the glass of water in front of her. "We gotta quit thinking that Houston's is a nice restaurant, that's all."

Black laughed his ass off. Then he sipped his water. The waitress appeared and they ordered drinks. Then TeTe ordered their food. Black trusted her since he'd never been there before. She ordered the roasted duck and Black had salmon and asparagus.

When the waiter disappeared, Black said, "I want to say how sexy you look."

"I had to put on more make up than usual. Had to cover up the bruises from the air-bags."

"You still look incredible."

She smiled and placed her napkin in her lap and said, "Thank you. And remind me to give you your gun back."

"So what did you wanna talk about?"

"You know damn well why I wanted to talk to you. We did just get shot at the other day."

"I'm sorry. There is some things I have to tell you."

"You think?"

"There are people after me. People wanting to kill me."

She sighed and then took a big gulp of her water. "Tell me something I don't motherfucking know."

Black looked confused. Did she just curse him? They were talking calmly and now he was being cursed out.

"Why are you cussing?"

"Will you tell me what the fuck is going on?"

Black's leg throbbed a little as the hydrocodone wore off. He slid to the side of the booth and lifted his leg. "My ex-girlfriend got murdered."

"Okay."

"And there are some people out there that think I had something to do with it."

"Did you?"

"If I did, I'd already be in prison."

"Not necessarily."

"I swear to God I didn't." He looked TeTe directly in the eyes and she believed him.

"Why do they think you had something to do with it?"

"I don't have the best reputation on the streets."

"You've been known to hurt people?"

"Yes."

"But you didn't hurt her?"

"I didn't, but everybody loved Lani and so they think I killed her."

"So who were these people? Her family?"

"I don't know."

There was a long silence before she said, "You're leaving something out."

"Why do you say that?"

"I can tell."

"I don't know if I can trust you."

"Why?"

"I just met you."

"I'm no angel. You know that."

"Okay, I'm supposed to trust you."

TeTe laughed and said. "That's up to you."

"My mother is doing life in prison in South Carolina."

"I'm sorry but what does that have to do with me."

"I know the streets, better than most."

He did know that and that was part of her appeal.

She said, "My man's got twenty-five years in prison for drugs and white slavery charges."

"Butterfly's Dad?"

"Not him, but he's in prison too. I'm talking about the man that taught me everything I know. A man named Slick, the best hustler I ever witnessed."

"Two men in prison and you're out."

"I never sold drugs, but I've been in the county jail before for a year."

Black laughed and said, "What street cred you have, my dear."

"What the fuck ever, Black."

"Why do you want to know who did this so bad?"

"I need a motherfucking drink," she announced then flagged the server and ordered a Tom Collins.

Black adjusted his leg again before deciding to place it back on the floor. Then he said, "I'm sorry. I can't tell you too much."

"Look, I was in that car too and if they would have killed me, who would have taken care of Butterfly?"

"Are you going to the police if I tell you who I think was behind it?"

The server dropped the Tom Collins off at the table. TeTe downed it then ordered another. Then she lowered her voice and said, "Do I look like a snitch?"

"I don't know what a snitch looks like."

"Well, I'm not."

"Look, my ex had a man named Shakur that I think had something do with it."

"Shakur?"

"Like in Tupac, but I think Shakur is his first name."

"Okay. I don't know anyone by that name."

"And then there is a dude named Mike that thinks I killed his brother," Black said. That was all he was going to tell her because he didn't want her to figure out that Chris was Lani's boyfriend too. He'd figured he told her too much already but what reason would she have to go to the cops and if she did, she didn't have the whole story.

"Mike?"

"Yeah."

"There is a million Mike's in Atlanta."

"Exactly."

"How was his brother murdered?"

"I don't know. His body was found in the trunk of a Lincoln, burned-up to a crisp."

"What was his last name?

"Why?"

"Just wanna know."

"Jones, I think."

"Chris Jones." TeTe said. "That name sounds so common."

"It is."

"And they think you did it?"

Black said, "I don't have the best reputation."

"So I've been hanging out with a killer."

"I wouldn't say all that."

"I wouldn't say all that either."

"What is that supposed to mean?"

"Do I think you're soft? No. Do I think you're a gangster? Hell no. I've been around real gangsters and you, my dear, are not a gangster."

"Damn."

"Just calling it like I see it."

The server brought the Tom Collins along with the rest of the food.

TeTe downed her drink and said, "I wish I knew who did this to us."

"It's okay, babe. We're here and we're safe."

"All glory be to God," she said then ordered another Tom Collins. She then made her way over to the other side of the booth and licked his ear, "I wish I'd worn a dress."

"Why?"

"So you could fuck me in the car."

Chapter 13

WHEN BLACK LIMPED DOWN INTO THE BASEMENT, HE FOUND L AND Avant holding hands, watching TV. Avant was wearing a hot-pink thong. A bag of buttered popcorn sat between them and there was a plasma TV on a stand. Avant's hands and feet were shackled.

"L, what the fuck are you doing?" Black said.

"Watching TV. What do it look like I'm doing?"

"Let me talk to you for a moment."

L stood up and then leaned forward and tongue kissed Avant. Then he trailed a wobbling Black up to the top of the stairs.

L said, "What the fuck happened to your leg?"

"I don't feel like talking about that right now."

"Look, man, I know you're tripping cuz I brought a TV and I'm down there watching it with him."

"That's not the point."

"What is the point?"

"You're getting too close to him."

"You want me here watching him twenty-four seven like I'm in prison or something but you don't want me to have no affection?"

"I ain't down with homosexual activities, but I couldn't care less what you do. I mean, I can't be here to watch you."

"What are your worries then?"

"You're getting a little too friendly."

"I'm getting paid to do a job. I don't understand why we just don't kill the motherfucker like Kyrie?"

L had a valid question and the only thing that separated Kyrie from Avant was that Kyrie ratted and Avant hadn't. Also, it wasn't Avant's idea to kill Lani. Avant didn't know Lani, but Black still wanted him to suffer. Black still hadn't decided if he was going to kill Avant or not, but in a sick kind of way, and even though he wasn't down with homosexuality, he was glad Avant was getting torture fucked by L.

Black said, "Just don't get too friendly with him."

L said, "Black, I would never betray you. I know what you think about me liking to fuck faggots. I never wanted you to find out about that. I really didn't. That's why I wanted to kill that dude in the park that day. I respect you and you're the last person I wanted to find out. I know you ain't down with that gay shit and I'm sorry that I let you down. I've been trying to leave it alone, but you know this is something that's in me. I guess Fy-Head was right. This is the real me. I thought when I got out that I could find me a woman and leave that shit behind in the pen, but the cravings came back and I just can't resist who I am."

Tears cascaded down the big man's face and Black felt sorry for him, but honestly he didn't give a damn about what L's sexuality was. He knew L was a killer and that was all he cared about.

Black hugged L and said, "It's all right, man."

Tears still rolled down L's face, and he said, "So, are you going to tell me what happened to your leg?"

"Somebody shot at me and I totaled my Porsche."

"Who? You know you my dawg, bruh. Just tell me who shot at you and I will handle that. Bruh, you know you my brother, and I'll die for you if I have to."

Black knew what L said was true and he knew that if L had an idea who had actually done this, there would be hell to pay. Revenge was on Black's mind but not as much as getting paid. His money was tied up with investments and he had to make some cash.

• • •

Jada opened the door and saw Fresh standing there. She was smiling hard as hell at the sight of him.

He said, "I got you a surprise."

She beamed even brighter. He held his hands behind his back and Jada tried to peek around him to see what he was holding.

"I loved surprises."

"Guess."

"A handbag?"

"Nope."

"Shoes?"

"Nope." He grinned and said, "You get one more guess."

"I don't know. A bracelet?"

"Nope, but you were close." Then he presented her with a little blue box from Blue Nile.

Jada beamed with excitement. She opened the box and laid her eyes on the earrings.

She bear hugged him and said, "Damn. I was just looking at this about six months ago."

"Dreams come true."

"They sure do." She smiled and led him into the house, and when they were seated she asked, "How long are you here for now?"

"Two weeks."

She made a sad face.

"Why the sad face, baby? That's a long time."

"I wish you could stay longer."

"I told you I'm thinking of getting me a place here."

"Let me know. I can find you something."

"For sure."

"I'm so glad you're here."

"Me too."

"Your boy got shot at the other day and totaled his Porsche."

Fresh knew she could only be speaking of Black. He didn't know of anybody else in Atlanta that they both knew except Starr. "Who shot at him?"

"He don't know."

"He must have some idea."

"Well, it could be Lani's ex or her other ex's brother."

"I gotta be careful around him."

"I don't want you hanging out with him."

"Okay, mama."

"Can you promise me that?"

"Hey, I won't."

Jada was still admiring the new earrings he'd brought and thinking that Fresh was definitely the kind of man that she could see herself with. Gangster and generous.

"I really love this."

"I tried my best."

She smiled and said, "You did and I want to thank you."

She made her way to where he sat and unzipped his pants and took him deep in her mouth. Suddenly, her phone rang. She removed it from her pocket and continued to deep throat Fresh while glancing at the phone. Unknown number. She figured it must be Shamari. She sent him to voicemail.

Chapter 14

JADA ENTERED THE VISITING ROOM OF THE UNITED STATES PRISON Atlanta. She heard one of the male prison guards say, "You gotta be a drug dealer or an athlete to have a woman that fine."

Jada rolled her eyes at the prison guard with the creased prison uniform. There was nothing worse than a broke-ass lame clown trying to holla. She sat at the table waiting on Shamari to come. The visitation room was eighty percent black and every black man in the visitation room, with the exception of two gay men, was looking in her direction with a look in their eyes that let her know that they would fuck her like a wild animal.

She glanced at her watch and mumbled that Shamari needed to hurry the fuck up. Seconds later, she spotted him strolling toward her in a khaki uniform and some Nikes that he'd gotten from the commissary. His yellow skin glowed, and he was buff from doing pull-ups and push-ups. Jada had to admit the motherfucker was fine as hell. And though she'd just fucked Fresh last night, she missed Shamari's ass.

She stood and hugged him.

"You know I wanna grab that ass, don't you?" he whispered.

She smiled before saying, "I want you to."

"They'll suspend my visit."

"Don't do it then."

He laughed before having a seat. Even though her clothing was baggy because of visitation guidelines, her figure was still on full display.

She took a seat and he said, "Glad you came."

"You didn't think I was coming?"

"You hardly answer the phone."

"Look, I know I've been a little busy, but please, don't think I've been avoiding you, baby. That's not it."

"I never said that."

"You were probably thinking it."

He was quiet. He didn't want to believe that she was probably fucking somebody else, but he was realistic about the situation.

"What's wrong, baby?"

"Your hair's different?"

"You like it?"

"I do like it. You never wore it like that for me."

"I know. I was just experimenting with it."

"Who you trying to impress?"

"Excuse me?"

"Who are you trying to impress?"

"My damn self."

"Who's been pulling on your hair?"

"Nobody," she lied. Fresh had been pulling on her hair as he fucked her doggy-style just last night, but he didn't need to know that.

"Who are you seeing?"

"Nobody."

"You don't answer the phone, Jada."

"What the fuck is this? An interrogation?" Jada whipped her hair over her shoulder, irritated as hell.

"Let me just stay in the moment. I really do appreciate you coming to see me. It's hell in there."

"Ain't nobody been fucking you?"

"No." He laughed. "You know I can handle myself. I mean, prison is not where it's at. You know the first time I was in state prison, I knew I was going home. Right now, I have no release date and some days that shit really bothers me."

"I know, baby. You tell me what you want me to do, and I'll do whatever it takes to get you out."

"There is no way I'm going to get out."

"We'll get another lawyer to find some loopholes. There has to be something we can do."

"I'm just lucky I didn't get the death penalty."

"I'm so glad Black came through for you."

"How is he doing?"

"He came over the other day."

Shamari said, "Why does he keep visiting. What does he want?"

"You think I would fuck Black? You can't be serious. Actually, one time he came over for you. Saying that you had reached out to him asking about me, so he came over to check on me for you."

"Look, I'm just asking you a question. No need to get all bent out of shape."

An inmate with gray cornrows, carrying a Polaroid camera, approached the table. "What about a picture of you and your girl?"

"Not right now," Shamari said.

The man eased away but not before stealing a glance at Jada's boobies.

"Look, out of respect for you and for my dead sister, Lani—"

"Lani is not your sister."

"We were like sisters. I would never fuck anybody she's had. Before Lani died, she was seeing this fine-ass nigga named Shakur. Tall, over six foot tall, and a body to die for, but I would never, ever, fuck even him and you think I would fuck Black. Who I know you were close to."

He sat there in silence. Their eyes met and held. Jada was unflinching and he believed her.

"Look, I'm sorry."

"Look, baby..." She rubbed his hands and he pulled back.

"So I can't touch you?"

"They will suspend my visit. You know you only get one hug in the beginning of the visit and one hug at the end."

"My bad." She paused and then said, "Look, I'm sorry that you're in here but it's not my fault."

There was a long awkward stare between them and then he said, "You're all I've got and I don't want to lose you."

"Oh, baby. You're never going to lose me," Jada said. Fresh had total control of her body but her loyalty was with Shamari.

Chapter 15

FRESH HAD JUST GOTTEN OUT OF THE SHOWER AND AFTER HE HAD lotioned up, he slid out of the bathroom. From his penthouse suite in the W, he looked at the Mayfair building across the street. He would have to make it a point to check out the building the next time to see what the amenities were like. He liked the area and Midtown seemed like a perfect location for him.

Black tapped on the door. When Fresh opened the door, he gave Black a pound and then spotted the cast.

"What happened to your leg?" he said.

"Jada didn't tell you?"

"I wanna hear your version. You know chicks can be so dramatic."

Fresh led Black to the living room area of the spacious suite. Black grabbed an apple from a bowl in the center of the table and bit into it.

"So, what happened?" Fresh asked again.

"Got shot at and I crashed my car trying to get away."

"You have enemies?"

"Don't we all?"

"I suppose so."

"This has nothing to do with you. If you decide to work with me, you'll get all your money."

"What do you mean by that? If I decide to work with you, I'll get all my money?"

"I need consignment."

"You're broke?"

"No. It's tied up. I invested in some restaurants."

Fresh stood and strolled over to the other side of the room before pulling the drapes back slightly. He glanced out at the Atlanta skyline.

"How much can you come up with?" Fresh asked.

"How much do I need?"

"A hundred thousand."

"So Trey was buying all his work?"

"I knew Trey, but I never dealt with Trey. He's actually a friend of my partners. What does Trey have to do with us? Trey's dead."

"Word in the streets was Trey had a connect in Houston that was fronting him all the work."

Fresh lit a cigar, then asked, "Do you mind if I smoke this?"

"I don't."

"I have more work than you'll ever need, but I can't just give you my shit. I don't know you. Just come up with some money and I'll take care of you."

"What's the ticket?"

"Twenty-two."

"That's a little high."

"Really, I don't think so. I sell for twenty-eight all day in Houston and I know you can get forty over here on the east coast. Actually, that's a deal."

What Fresh was saying was true, but Black didn't know that Fresh actually knew the prices for coke in Atlanta. He would come up with the money somehow. He'd made great money with the heroin, but there was too much to worry about. Too many people OD'ing and it had made his job harder than it needed to be.

"You want a hundred grand?"

"If you can come up with it."

"Why not eighty-eight? That way I can buy four."

"Give me a hundred grand and I'll give you two hundred grand in inventory. Give me a hundred thousand and I'll give you ten ki's. You can pay me the rest on the back end.

Fair?"

"More than fair."

• • •

It was nine thirty at night and Sasha was lying on the sofa crying when Black walked into her house. She was crying so hard that she didn't notice Black walk in.

He startled her when he asked, "What are you crying for? What's wrong?" He sat in the chair on the other side of the coffee table.

She sat up and grabbed a tissue from the table. "I don't wanna burden you with my problems."

"You're my friend."

She avoided his eyes.

"What happened?"

Silence.

"How is business?"

"Better than imagined."

"So what's wrong?"

She was quiet again and Black searched her eyes trying to find clues. She stood and Black noticed that she was commando underneath the big T-shirt she was wearing and then it hit him—the smell of sex.

"He touched you again."

She reached for another tissue and said, "I don't want to talk about it."

She was easing her way into the kitchen and Black followed her. She grabbed a wine cooler from the fridge and passed it to him to twist the top off for her. He used his shirt to get a grip and twisted it off with one motion then passed it back.

"Look, don't lie to me. He's touched you again."

"What if he did? I mean what are you going to do about it? Confront him? Tell him to stop? Kill him? He's the mayor of the goddamn city and you're just a—." She stopped.

"I'm just a D-Boy. Go ahead and say it. I'm a hood-ass nigga that you think you're too good for. That's what you want to say, princess? I tell you what? I might have come from the slums, and my daddy might have been a drug dealer too, but what your daddy is doing is wrong."

She looked at him with sad eyes. "Who am I going to go to? What am I going to do?"

"You're a grown woman. You can't let this man keep doing this to you."

"I know."

"If you know, why do you keep giving in to him?"

"I don't know."

"Do you like it?"

There was a long pause and the she took a swig from her bottle and said, "I don't know."

Chapter 16

STARR HAD BEEN CALLING Q FOR THE PAST TWO DAYS AND HIS PHONE was going straight to voicemail. She wanted to go to his building to see what was going on, but decided against it. Instead, she called Jada and asked her to meet her for Mimosas. Starr noticed Jada's earrings and said, "I love your new earrings."

Jada smiled and said, "Fresh got them for me."

"When is the last time you talked to him?"

"A few minutes ago."

"When is he coming back to the A?"

"He's here."

"Huh?"

"Yeah, he's been here for a couple of days now. Q didn't tell you?"

"I haven't spoken to Q in a while. He hasn't called me or returned my text."

"I didn't know. Perhaps he's busy."

"Maybe." Now Starr was pissed the fuck off. She'd been calling that motherfucker and he hadn't answered her. It was obvious that he was ignoring her and that wasn't cool to her at all.

Jada ordered another round of Mimosas and when the server dropped the drinks on the table, Jada said, "I think I'm falling for him, Starr."

Starr stared into space. Thinking about the fact that days had passed since the last time she'd spoken with Q. What was he doing? Was he seeing somebody else? What the fuck was going on?

Jada said, "Did you hear me?"

"No."

"I'm falling for him."

"Falling for who?"

"Fresh. Crazy girl."

Starr laughed and said, "I'm sorry, Jada. I was lost in thought. You say that you're falling for Fresh?"

"Yeah."

"What about Shamari?"

"I went to see him today. He's doing good, but the reality of it is that he's going to be gone for the rest of his life unless there is an act of God."

"Yeah, and that's sad. I always liked Shamari."

"I love Shamari. I'll always love Shamari and whoever I'm with is going to have to know that he'll always be a part of my life."

"You think they're going to understand that?"

Jada finished her Mimosa and said, "I don't know. I really can't answer that question."

"And Shamari? Do you think he will understand?"

"He's not understanding right now. But, sooner or later, he's going to understand. Reality will sink in."

"Right, Right," Starr said. Trying to stay engaged in the conversation. Trying her very best not to think about Q, but it was becoming difficult not to think about the fact that he'd been ignoring the fuck out of her.

"He accused me of fucking with Black."

"Who?"

"Shamari. Stay with me, Starr." Jada laughed because clearly her friend's mind was somewhere else.

"You can't be serious. Trifling-ass Black?" Starr said. Though she thought some of the things Jada did were a little out there, nobody was more trifling than Black.

"Yeah, can you believe that?"

"You know how dudes can be when they're locked up."

"I know, but it kind of hurt because you know I would never do that to Lani. Not to mention I ain't even attracted to Black's ass."

"I still can't believe Lani is gone."

Jada looked away and then she locked eyes with Starr again. "I know. I try my best not to think about it. I try to believe that she's still here. I still have her last voicemail in my phone. I listen to it sometimes. I have her number stored in my phone. I call it and I don't know why, but that phone is still on. Maybe her mom is paying the bill, I don't know. I call the phone sometimes and it goes to voicemail. And when I hear windshield wipers, it really fucks me up. That's the last thing I remember when she got gunned down—the sound of her wipers. Sometimes when it's not raining too hard, I don't turn my wipers on. It makes me so sad."

Starr was tearing up, Jada made her way to the other side of the booth and the women embraced. Starr turned to Jada and said, "I know I've never told you this, but I'm so glad to have you as a friend."

Jada held her tight.

• • •

His name was John Clyburn. He was a fifty-five-year-old black man with a graying mustache and a goatee. He was of average height and was the best damned private investigator in Atlanta. He stirred a latte at a table in Starbucks as he waited on TeTe. John was a good friend of TeTe's. Moments later, she arrived and John gave her a double European air kiss. He'd spent fifteen years in the military and the majority of that time he was stationed in Germany. As a result, he ended up adopting many of their customs.

He pulled her chair out for her and when they were seated, she said to him, "I need to find someone."

"If they can be found, I can find them."

"Mike Jones."

"Mike Jones?"

"Is that a problem?" TeTe asked.

"No, it's not a problem. The name is just so goddamned common. Hell, there was even a rapper named Mike Jones a few years ago.

TeTe laughed and said, "How in the hell did you know that?"

"I know everything." John laughed then added a creamer to his latte. "There is no way I can find anyone with just a name. I'm good, but I'm not that good."

"His brother's name is Chris Jones. He was killed about a year ago and his remains were found in the trunk of a car."

John was listening while using the stirrer to mix his coffee. He added two Splendas.

"You want what?"

"His brother's whereabouts."

John sipped his coffee quickly. "Damn, this is hot. When did this happen?"

"What?"

"The murder. When was the body found?"

"I don't know. Sometime last year."

John sat his coffee on the table and then scribbled down the names TeTe had given him on a legal pad. Then he asked, "Is this all you know about the murder?"

"That's all."

John said, "Just curious, what do you need this information for?"

"Are you going to tell anybody?"

"No."

"I want to ask the brother a few questions."

Do you want me to approach him?"

"No. I just need to know where I can find him."

"Ok, give me a week or so."

"A week or so? Why so long?"

"This is Atlanta. I'm sure there was more than one body found in a trunk last year."

"Okay. If you can find them fast, I would appreciate it."

"Them?"

"I mean him." Tee stood and extended her hand then asked, "What is this going to cost me?"

"You know what I like." John grinned, looking very much like the old pervert that he was.

"I got some new girls. There is this one half Japanese, half black girl I think you would like."

"How old is she?"

"Twenty-nine."

"Too old."

"Oh yeah, I forgot, you don't like nothing over twenty-three."

"Exactly."

"Find this guy and I'll get you two twenty-two year olds. I promise."

"He will be found, don't worry. It's just a matter of when I have time."

Chapter 17

STARR SHOWED UP AT Q'S BUILDING UNANNOUNCED AFTER SHE dropped T.J. off at school. Security buzzed Q and he told them to send her up. He opened the door wearing nothing but a bathrobe. He invited her in.

He said, "I'm sorry. I didn't know you were coming or else I would have made breakfast for you. I can order some food from the restaurant in the building if you want."

"Quentin, I'm not here to eat or play no damn games. You know why I'm here."

He didn't respond.

"Where the hell have you been?"

"I told you I was going to Houston."

"Yeah, but you've been back for a couple of days."

"I have."

"And I haven't heard from you."

He stood and he paced nervously and he said, "I got major shit to deal with right now."

"So you're phone doesn't work?"

"My phone works."

"Why didn't I get a call?"

He sat down on the arm of the sofa and said, "Because I felt guilty."

"Guilty? What the fuck do you mean guilty? So you're not feeling me no more? Do you have somebody else? Is that it?"

"There's nobody."

"What is there to feel guilty about?"

"Because I lied to you."

"About?"

"Look, I'm going to work again. I don't want to do it but I can't leave my friend there."

"Ok, that's no reason to feel guilty. You're a grown man. You can do what you damn well please."

"I know, but I told you that I was getting out."

"So, why ain't you getting out?"

"I know this sounds crazy to you, but this is something that I chose to do with my life and as crazy as it sounds, I don't think I can get out. If I get out of the business, they are going to kill me."

"What?"

"Look, I'm nobody's punk and I damn sure ain't afraid to die but I got children that I have to be there for. I can't let them down."

"So you going to have to keep dealing and possibly go to prison? Look, I was the girl whose father got sent to the Feds. I loved my daddy but I was so hurt when he went away."

"But he came back. He got out. Your dad is still here. Living. Breathing."

He had a point, and she knew her dad was never tied to the cartel. Even though he was big in Atlanta, he was small fish compared to Q. She thought Q would never get out if he were ever caught.

"So you're just going to keep dealing?"

"Supplying."

"Dealing. Supplying. It's all the same thing."

"I've got to get them to let my friend go. I have to get him back to his wife and kids."

"How do I know this is true?"

"You think I would lie about something like that?" Q was visibly angry and Starr had never heard him talk to her like that. He removed a phone from his pocket and presented her with pictures of Rico with his feet tied, looking extremely frail as if he hadn't eaten in days.

"What the fuck? What kind of people are these?"

"When I tell you that this is the cartel, I mean it. They don't play no games."

"But how are they going to just make you sell drugs?"

"They feel that they made me rich and so I owe them. But I had money before I even got involved with them."

"So they didn't make you rich?"

"They did. I told you, I have more money than I can count, more than I can ever use."

"So you're back in the business?"

"I have no choice. What would you do if they had one of your friend's hostage?"

Starr stood and made her way to the door. He stepped in front of her.

"Get out of my way, Quentin."

"Don't leave."

"I told you that I couldn't go through this again. I'm too old for this."

He leaned forward and took hold of her neck and she struggled to push him away, but he was too strong. He pressed his mouth against hers and she couldn't resist him. They kissed. He opened his robe and this was the first time that she'd seen him naked. Though he was older, he had an incredibly chiseled body. He removed the robe and his dick stood at attention through the white boxer briefs that were shellacked on his thighs and ass.

She kicked off her Uggs and removed her jeans. She was wearing yellow lace panties, a pink bra and Hello Kitty socks. Nothing matched and in her mind she felt she looked a hot mess but to him, she was absolutely breathtaking. It had been very cold this morning when she'd dropped T.J. off and she never thought anyone would see her, but now she was standing in Q's penthouse in just her panties and bra. He leaned into her and kissed her again. This time, he gripped her ass and she felt herself becoming wet. He scooped her up and carried her to the huge marble coffee table and lay her across it before ripping her bra off like an animal. He stared in admiration at her completely natural body and thought to himself that it was amazing that this girl didn't work out or hadn't had any work done. Her body was better than ninety-nine percent of the women he'd seen.

He removed her panties and saw her pussy hair was shaved in the shape of a triangle. She would usually have waxed, but since she hadn't been having sex, she saw no reason to subject herself to that kind of pain. He lowered his head between her legs and licked her pussy and she moaned. His mouth covered her clit and she wiggled a little before getting comfortable. He inserted his finger and finger-fucked her while licking her clit. Then he turned her over on her stomach.

She said, "This table is cold."

He ignored her and just took hold of her again. He handled her rough but gentle at the right time. He was a grown-ass man and she could tell that he was very skilled at lovemaking and fucking. He was exactly what she needed.

He placed her gently on the sofa and kissed her softly. He whispered, "I love you, Starr."

She didn't want to reveal that she loved him, but she couldn't help herself. "I love you, too."

He bit her neck and then sucked her nipples.

She said, "I want you inside of me." She reached for his dick. It was as hard as a piece of steel. Then she got on her knees and examined his dick. He had the thickest dick that she'd ever seen. So beautiful and veiny. The shaft was chocolate like ice cream and the head was pink like strawberry.

All she needed to do was make him explode so she could see the vanilla and she would have her Neapolitan. She started to suck his dick.

She looked up at him and he smiled. She knew that guys liked this for some reason. Perhaps they felt dominant. She sucked the head of his dick and licked the shaft while toying with his balls.

"You feel so, so good," he said.

He flipped her over on her stomach and entered her from behind. He yanked her hair and she loved that shit. The perfect gentleman that could fuck like a thug. He slapped her ass hard and she came on his dick. Seconds after she came, he came all over that big beautiful ass. She turned and she was on her knees again, slurping up every last drop of her vanilla ice cream. She had gotten her full serving of Neapolitan.

Chapter 18

WHEN BLACK ENTERED THE HOUSE, HE CALLED OUT TO L. NO response. He peeked inside the guest bedroom and spotted a backpack and two guns lying on the bed. L's shoes were under the bed, so he knew L was there. He figured L had to be in the basement with Avant. He was about to make his way to the basement but decided to take a peek inside the backpack. To Black's surprise, the backpack was full of cash. Stacks of money. He knew he didn't have any cash in the house, so where did L get this money? Whose money was it?

Black limped to the edge of the stairs. Crutches in hand, he didn't feel like going down those stairs. His leg had been bothering him. He stood on the edge of the stairway and yelled down. "L!?."

L was down in the basement sitting on a folding chair eating Flamin' Hot Cheetos and watching Breaking Bad. Avant was lying down on a blanket inside the cage facing the opposite side of the TV.

Black yelled, "L, what the fuck is going on, bruh?"

"Watching a little TV. What do you think I'm doing?"

"We need to talk."

L sat the bag of Cheetos down and ran upstairs to find Black standing with his crutches resting underneath his arm.

"Wassup?"

"Where did you get the money from?"

"Huh?"

"The money in your backpack."

"You've been searching through my shit?"

L licked the Cheetos residue from his hand and Black realized how big L's hand was. Black knew that if he and L were to fight at this point, he would have to slap the fuck out of him with his crutches.

"Where did the money come from, L?"

"It's not your money."

"I know it's not my money."

"So what difference does it make?"

"I know you've never had that kind of money in your life."

"Well, now I do." He grinned. "Look, you asked me to do a job and I've been doing a damn good job."

"You have, but why can't you tell me where the money came from?"

L looked away. He was trying to think up a good story. A good lie. A good reason for the money but at the last minute he said, "Look, I took the money from someone."

"I know."

L looked confused. "Why do you care?"

"Well, you are staying in my house, L. So, who did you get the money from?"

"D-Boys that Avant knew."

"You robbed them?"

"Why the fuck not?. Look, man, I ain't never had shit in my life, and here's my chance to come up. Why can't I shine?"

"L, you're forty-five. Damn near fifteen years older than me. You are too old to be acting like this."

"I've been in prison all my life. I wanna win sometimes. And why do you have to be the one with all the money? You're just happy with me being your fucking flunky."

Black knew that L was getting out of hand, and that he needed to get rid of L. He didn't want to kill him, he liked L, but L was becoming too reckless.

"Look, L. That was something you shouldn't have done."

"Do you want half the money? It's yours if you want it, bruh. I'm not like that. If I got it, you got it."

"L, that is not the point."

"Help me understand the point."

"We have a man in my basement."

"A man that I brought here."

"Look, L, the point is that I don't want you to do anything stupid. I don't need you robbing anybody else."

"I can dig it."

"Can you really?"

"Look, I won't do it again. I have more money than I've had in my life."

Black stared at L for a long time. His lips were orange from those Flamin' Cheetos. He wanted to cut L out, but L knew too much about him.

• • •

When Fresh woke up, he realized that he was in Jada's bed, but she wasn't there. He stood up from the bed and headed to the bathroom to take a pee. He washed his hands and brushed his teeth with the toothbrush that Jada had given him the last time he was there.

He was staring in the mirror when she burst into the bathroom and said, "Damn, baby, you're so sexy."

"You think so?"

"You know what turns me on?"

"What?"

She smiled and said. "First, you have to promise not to laugh at me."

"What turns you on?"

"Your doo-rag. I don't know why. I think I have a doo-rag fetish."

He laughed, but then he said, "You know that's not actually that weird. I knew another girl that used to say that."

"Well, she better stay away now."

"Is that so?"

"Oh, don't let the good looks fool you. I'm known to beat a bitch down."

"I believe that."

"You better. So you better tell all your other bitches to stay away."

"What's for breakfast?"

Jada wrapped her arms around him and bit softly on his ear. "What did you say?"

"Breakfast."

"Oh, mama hooked you up. I fried eggs and turkey bacon, toast. And cereal. I didn't know if you was the type that ate turkey bacon or if you like swine, so I gave you turkey bacon. I'm a Georgia peach, born and raised, so I ain't gonna lie, I prefer swine, but lately I've been rocking with the turkey bacon."

"I like turkey bacon too."

"But you know, I think they be lying cuz some of that shit taste like pork. How in the fuck do they do that?"

"I don't know, babe."

Her hands were now caressing his abs and then she took hold of his dick and said, "Can I get some of this for dessert?"

"No. Tonight, I promise. I got a lot to do today."

"How in the hell do you have a lot to do in Atlanta? You ain't even from here."

She released him and he removed his doo-rag and brushed his hair. Then he followed her into the dining room, where their plates were waiting on them.

"So what do you have going on today?"

"Business."

"I know that."

He snatched the strawberry jam from the center of the table and spread some on his toast, and then he bit into it. Jada just sat watching him. She enjoyed watching him. She hadn't felt like this in a very long time.

"So, what do you think about the food?"

"The best damn toast I've ever eaten."

"Fuck you, asshole," she said, laughing.

"What do you want me to say? I've only eaten the toast."

"I want you to say it looks amazing. I'm sure it's amazing."

"It looks amazing. I'm sure the food tastes amazing."

"You know what? You got jokes."

He ate a forkful of eggs and then the bacon and said, "Okay, at least I know that my future wife can make bacon and eggs."

"Future wife?"

"Just kidding."

"Don't kid like that."

"My bad. Don't you want to be a wife one day?"

"I do. I didn't think I would ever want to be somebody's wife, and I know I'm making myself vulnerable, but fuck it, I like you a lot, Fresh."

"I like you."

She bit into her toast and said, "No, I don't think you understand. I really like you."

There was an awkward silence. He ate his bacon and eggs.

Finally, she said, "I don't expect you to marry me, Fresh. I was just letting you know how I feel."

"I know."

"You got so damn quiet."

"I'm sorry, baby. My mind was somewhere else," he lied. He was thinking about what she had just said. He liked her but it was clear to him that she liked him more than he liked her at this point. But he did think Jada was the kind of woman he could see himself with, but right now, he didn't feel that way.

"I want to ask you a question."

She took a swig of orange juice and said, "I'm listening."

"What do you think about Black?"

"I've already told you how I feel about Black."

"I know. I guess I'm looking for you to convince me one way or the other whether to fuck with him."

"Look, you're a grown man. You do what you want to do. I've already told you that Black has enemies, but he does good business for the most part."

"The most part?"

"He's greedy as hell.,"

"Aren't we all?"

"Do what you want to do with Black, but if it blows up in your face, don't say shit to me."

"Do you think it will blow up in my face?"

"I don't know."

"Is Black the reason Shamari is in prison?"

"No. Shamari is the reason he is in prison."

"How did Black escape?"

"Nobody wanted to testify on him. His friends took the fall for him. He has loyal friends. Black is no snitch, I can tell you that. Though he did tell the Feds where a body was to keep Shamari from getting the death penalty."

"He did that?"

"Yeah."

"Damn. Tell me about it."

"I don't want to get into it."

He stood up and made his way over to her. He planted a kiss on her jaw before heading out the door. She had fallen for him, and it had become apparent that he didn't feel the same way. She watched him walk out of the door. She hated feeling this way, but she couldn't help it.

Chapter 19

WHEN BLACK HOBBLED ON CRUTCHES INTO FRESH'S HOTEL SUITE, there was strange man there. A tall guy wearing expensive jeans, a T-shirt and a Frank Mueller watch that Black had priced at around fifty grand. The man looked to be in his early to late thirties. He looked like money.

The stranger introduced himself. "I'm Q."

Fresh said, "This is my partner."

Black and Q shook hands. Q handed Black a pair of shorts and ordered him to go change.

Black stared at the shorts, a yellow pair of Nautica swimming trunks.

"What do you mean, go change into these?"

Q said, "Relax. Just want to protect ourselves."

"You think I'm wearing a wire?"

"I didn't say that."

Black looked at the small-ass shorts that he was sure would cling to his ass like a pair of Daisy Dukes. He didn't want to put them on, but he complied.

When he entered the restroom, Q said, "Leave your phone in the bathroom and turn the shower on."

"Okay."

Moments later, Black remerged into the suite and found Q and Fresh sitting at the table.

Q said, "You knew Trey?"

"I did."

"You ever do business with him?"
"Once, but I vaguely remember."
"You sell heroin too?"
"For a while, but I'm not doing anything now."
"Coke and heroin are different."
"Look, I know the coke business. My dad was once the biggest coke dealer in Atlanta."
"No open cases."
"None."
Q said, "Just so you know. I don't take losses."
"Huh?"
"Meaning if I give you something, I expect to get paid."
"You will."
"I can make you a rich man."
"I already got money."
"Fresh said you didn't have a hundred thousand."
"My money is tied up."
"Meaning you don't have money."
"I guess not."
Fresh said, "How fast can you get rid of a hundred ki's?"
"I know I can do that in at least a month."
Fresh and Q laughed and said, "A month?"
"Yeah, I'm fast."
"We're thinking that's actually slow."
"A hundred kilos a month is slow? How many did you used to give Trey?"
"Not much, but Trey was buying his own shit, so he could do whatever he wanted; however he wanted."
"I see."
Fresh said, "How much money do you have?"
"I was able to come up with fifty grand."
"I needed a hundred."
"I don't have it right now," Black said.
Black suddenly became self-conscious about being damn near naked with two men in a hotel room. But he understood exactly why this made them feel comfortable. They didn't know him.
"Give us an address. I'll have something delivered to you."
Fresh passed Black the hotel pen and pad, and Black scribbled Nana's address on the paper.
"This is my grandma's house, so you make sure you wrap it up nice."
"You telling me how to do my job?" Q said."
"No, bruh."
"Look, we're going to take care of this. Don't worry."
Fresh said, "I thought you were a major player in Atlanta."
"I do okay for myself."
"We need you to do more than okay. We need people to do volume. To be

honest, this is a waste of time."

They'd just made Black feel small as hell. He did what he could do. He knew that he wasn't the biggest dope dealer in Atlanta, but he thought he did well for himself.

Black stood and was about to head to the bathroom to change back into his clothes when Q said, "Black?"

"Yeah?"

"Are you cut out for this?"

"Homie, if I get caught, I can do my time."

"Not talking about getting caught. Only dumb hustlers get caught."

"I'm saying you're going to be in the big leagues. A different level of money. A different level of access. We don't need you to do nothing stupid."

"Bruh," Black said, then he smiled, "I'm good. I might not have your money, but it ain't like you dealing with a peasant."

They all laughed their asses off then Black went into the bathroom and got his clothes and cell phone. He re-emerged, gave Fresh and Q a pound, and then left. An hour later, Nana called and told him that some man had dropped off a plasma TV. When Black opened the box, it had ten kilos of coke with a handwritten note from Q saying it was nice meeting him today.

• • •

Fresh received another text from Diego. Three days. He showed Q the text.

"What the fuck?"

"There is no way we're going to get rid of two thousand kilos in three days," Fresh said.

"We can do a thousand though."

"A thousand won't do. They're going to kill him."

"We're going to have to go into our stash and pay the rest. Then get our money on the back end."

"You want to pay for a thousand kilos?" Fresh asked.

"If we can sell a thousand, then we can pay for the other thousand."

"This is complete bullshit. How in the fuck does he think he can make somebody work for him?"

"You knew he hated Rico."

"We always send Rico. What the fuck are you talking about?," Fresh said.

Fresh was right and Q knew it. They'd always sent Rico. "We're going to have to pay out of our pockets."

Q passed the phone back to Fresh and Fresh brought the calculator up on the phone. He calculated the cost of 1000 ki's at 10,000 each and then he said, "Do you realize that you're talking about paying ten million dollars?"

"I didn't realize it was that much," Q said. "But I'll pay half and you pay half."

"I don't have five million dollars, bruh."

"Do you have three?"

"No."

"What the fuck have you been doing with your money?"

"I've been spending it. I'm a young nigga."

"Now you're young. A couple of weeks ago, I said I was old and you're young."

"Look, I spend a lot of money. Don't talk to me like you're my daddy."

"If I got to send ten million dollars to Diego, then you're not going to see any profit because I got to put my shit up."

An image came through on Fresh's phone. A butt naked picture of Rico lassoed and gagged.

Then Rico's daughter Ivy texted: *Still haven't seen my Dad*?

"Let me make some phone calls quickly."

Chapter 20

JOHN CALLED TETE AND GAVE HER THE INFORMATION ON MICHAEL Jones that she needed. Michael had a place in Buckhead but his primary residence was with his wife and seven-year-old son.

TeTe had her goons, Todd and Dank, stake out Mike's house for twenty-four hours and they never saw Mike. All they observed were a woman and a little boy going in and out of the house. On the third day, they saw a black man that looked like the guy in the picture that John had given TeTe. The next morning they parked a white work van in the driveway of a rental house on the opposite end of the street. They sat in the van eating Egg McMuffins and potatoes and sipping Cokes.

Todd said, "Remember not to hurt the woman and the kid. As a matter of fact, I'll take care of them.

Dank smacked loudly as he ate his Egg McMuffin, and it irritated the fuck out of Todd. He stuffed some potatoes in his mouth before removing the lid off the coke and burped. "I know what she told us and what she told us was nobody was going to get hurt. Not just the woman and kid."

"She said nobody is to get hurt at the house. Especially the woman and kid."

"As long as the motherfucker does what he's told, nobody has to get hurt."

Todd sipped his soda and watched the house with a pair of high-powered binoculars. He noticed that the woman and her son were coming out of the house. He quickly drove down the street, pulling up in front of her. When he made eye contact with the woman, he lowered the window of the van and asked, "Do you know where Shadow Lane is?"

"What street?" She ordered her son to get in the family car as she approached the strange men.

Todd held a map to his face and said, "Yeah I'm looking for Shadow Lane. According to this map, it should be around here."

"Can I see the map? Maybe I can help you out."

Todd lowered the map and the woman spotted the Desert Eagle. She was about to scream and Todd said, "Make one sound and I will blow your goddamned head off, you hear me?"

Her heart was trying to burst through her chest. She breathed hard and quick.

Todd and Dank exited the van and walked her over to her car. She ordered her son to get out of the car. Greedy ass Dank still carrying the bag of food finished off his potatoes then tossed the McDonalds bag in the yard then yanked the little boy out of the car and covered his mouth and they walked quickly toward the house. The woman struggled to open the door before Todd slapped her twice in the back of the head with the gun and said. "Open this goddamned door or I'm killing yo ass! "She opened the door fast and then they disappeared into the house before the neighbors could see them.

Inside the house, Mike was lying in the bedroom sprawled across the bed, asleep with his mouth open.

Dank slapped Mike hard as fuck in the mouth with the gun. "Wake up, bitch!"

Mike came to and tried to focus on the two goons in his bedroom. Why were they here and how did they get in his house?

"Sit up," Dank said.

Todd followed Mike's eyes to a chrome Taurus 9.mm on the nightstand. Todd grabbed the gun and said, "Mike, you're going to do what the fuck we say. You understand me?"

"What do you want? You want money? You want work?"

"I want you to know that the person that you shot at the other day was a very important person. Do you understand me?"

"What are you talking about?"

"Mike, you're going to cooperate with us. Understand? Either you cooperate or your baby mama and your son will be found in the fucking ocean somewhere."

"What do you want?"

Dank sat down on the edge of the bed, his gun pointing at Mike. Mike knew by the size of the gun that it had to be a Desert Eagle or something. Dank ordered Todd to take the woman and the kid to the other room. When he heard the door close, he said, "This is the deal we're going to make. You're going to let me know where these other men are and your son and wife live."

"If I don't?"

Dank slapped the fuck out of Mike with the gun and said, "You're not that motherfuckin' stupid. If you don't tell me who those other men are, we're going to end your life, your kid's life and your wife's life. Am I clear?"

"And if I do?"

"I hate repeating my motherfucking self. They live."

"And me?"

"It's over for you. It's just a matter of if you have balls enough to spare your family."

Dank ordered Todd to bring the woman and the kid into the room. Mike stared at his son standing there with his jacket on. He was still wearing his little Spiderman backpack. He stood and made his way over to his son.

"Dad, save us from the bad guys," his son said.

Mike kissed his son on his forehead and said, "I love you, son."

"If you love me, you'll save us from the bad guys."

"I do love you, son."

Dank said, "Get the kid out of here!" Then Dank turned to Mike. "What are you going to do?"

"I'm gonna call the other men."

"Smart guy."

"What about my wife and kid?"

"They'll live."

"How do I know you're going to do what you said you're going to do?"

"Because I said I was, and that's the only thing that you're going to have to go on."

"So I have to take your word for it?"

"What motherfucking choice do you have?"

"None."

"Exactly."

Mike got dressed and phoned Kenny-Boo and Tater, asking them to come over. Tater came over first and screamed like a bitch when he opened the door and saw the Desert Eagle pointed at him.

"Oh God! Oh God!" Tater screamed.

"You're going to see him soon enough," Todd said.

Tater spotted Mike tied up in the corner and wondered who in the hell the man pointing the gun at his head was. Was this a robbery?

Dank grabbed Tater's ass and flung him to the floor. Tater struggled, kicking and spitting while clawing at the carpet. He thought about making a dash for the door but when he stood up, Dank kicked him in the stomach. Tater fell face down on the floor and then Dank smacked him in the mouth with the gun. Dank then gagged and hogtied Tater's bitch ass.

Ten minutes later, Kenny-Boo rolled in. As soon as Kenny saw the gun, he tried to run out the door but was tackled by Todd. Todd cuffed and dragged him into the room with Mike and Tater.

"Mike, what the fuck is going on?" Kenny-Boo asked.

Mike couldn't answer. He was gagged and tears were cascading down his face. He was wondering who the fuck these men in his house were, and what were they going to do with him. He suspected that Black must have had something to do with this.

Todd phoned TeTe. "I got them. We got all three of them and we'll bring them to you tonight when the sun goes down. We don't want to take a chance and have one of the neighbors spot us and call the police.

"Tonight, then. You're at Mike's house?"

"Yeah."

"All three?"

"Yes."

"Is any of them named Shakur?"

Todd turned and said, "Who is Shakur?"

No one moved.

"None of them is named Shakur."

"Check their licenses."

Kenny Boo's license said Kenny McDonald and Tater's license read Shawn Wright.

"Nobody is named Shakur." Todd pulled the gag off Mike and asked, "Who the fuck is Shakur?"

"I know him, but we ain't friends."

"You know where he lives?"

"No, he don't fuck with me. We had a disagreement."

TeTe could hear the conversation on the phone and she said, "Meet me in Dunwoody and make sure nobody has a phone on them."

"Huh?"

"Do what I say."

• • •

Later that evening, they met TeTe in a home that she rented in Dunwoody. All three men were gagged and bound. TeTe, wearing a business suit and basic black Louboutin shoes, stood over the men. She was dressed very conservatively and none of the men knew who the fuck she was. They were hogtied and laying on the carpeted floor while she paced in front of them.

"I bet ya'll wondering why in the fuck are ya'll here and who in the fuck am I?"

She asked Dank, "Which one of these characters' name is Mike?"

He pointed to Mike who was feeling like a bitch for giving up his friends, but it was either them or his wife and child.

"Untie him."

Dank untied Mike, and TeTe said, "Come here, Mike."

Mike approached.

"Bow."

"Huh?"

"Bow! I need you to bow down. You're in the presence of a queen."

Mike was thinking was this crazy bitch serious. Did she really think she was a queen? Dank now had the Desert Eagle a hair away from his temple. He screamed that he had heard her and bowed.

TeTe said, "I need you on your knees when you're talking to me."

Mike plummeted to his knees.

"I know you're wondering who the fuck I am."

Mike shook his head.

"I was in the car that you shot at."

"I didn't shoot at nobody."

"Mike, don't play with my motherfucking intelligence."

"I don't even know you."

"Where the fuck is Shakur?" TeTe said. Then, very calmly, she said, "Dank tells me you have a cute little boy."

"Please, leave my son out of this. I'll do whatever you want me to do."

"I'm going to make you a deal, Mike."

"What kind of deal?"

"Do you want to raise that little boy of yours?"

Mike said, "Why should I believe you now? You said that you were going to let my son and wife live once I gave you my friends." Mike turned to his friends and though they were gagged, he could see the disappointment in their eyes. He'd proven to be a bitch-ass nigga to them, but he didn't have a choice.

"Your son and wife are going to be okay."

"So why do want to make another deal?"

"Will you shut the fuck up!"

Mike was quiet, thinking he would smack the fuck out this bitch if it weren't for the clown pointing the gun at his head. One thing he never liked was a chick who thought she was a man, and this chick was clearly that.

TeTe walked closer to Mike, who was down on his hands and knees. She stepped on his hand. The Louboutin heel dug deep into the backside of his hand. He grimaced but he didn't scream like he wanted to at that moment.

"Now I'm going to need you to shut the fuck up for few moments. Understand me?"

"Yes, can you take your foot off my hand?"

"Say pretty please."

Was she serious?

TeTe laughed at him and spiked her heel deeper into his flesh until he screamed.

"Pretty please!" he cried.

She removed her heel and Mike stared at his throbbing hand as it bled.

"I need Shakur."

"I don't know how to get in touch with him. I have his number but I don't have my phone."

"Look, one of ya'll were responsible for shooting at a car that I was in and I intend to find out who."

TeTe looked at Dank. "Call Todd and tell him to power on Mike's phone and find Shakur's number."

Dank called and Mike informed him that his phone was the new iPhone 6. Todd found Shakur's number in the contacts and gave it to Dank.

TeTe said, "Tell Todd to take a picture of the kid and send it to me."

Seconds later, a picture of Mike's kid came to TeTe's phone.

She presented Mike the picture of his son sitting on the sofa. "You see? He's okay."

"Thank God."

"Seven or eight?"

"Seven."

"My daughter is eight. She's my world."

Mike didn't know if he should say something about his son or not. This seemed a little odd, but the picture of his son made him feel like he should at least try to call Shakur. If there was a chance that he could ever see his son again, he would have to do it.

She passed him her phone and Dank called the number out.

"I need you to call Shakur," TeTe said.

"He's not going to answer."

"Do what I say."

He dialed the number. "No answer."

"Try again."

He tried again.

Shakur said, "Hello?"

"This is Mike."

"What the fuck do you want?"

"I need to talk. Can I meet up with you?

"I'm at L.A Fitness on Piedmont. If you want to talk, come to the gym."

"Okay." He terminated the call then said to TeTe, "He's at the gym. He's not going to meet me."

"That's okay" You can give us a description of him and Dank will go check him out. We'll get back to his ass sooner or later. "

Chapter 21

Q AND FRESH HAD GOTTEN RID OF A THOUSAND KILOS IN TWO DAYS. They had given the Virginia, North Carolina and Louisiana distributors the majority of the drugs. Q's longstanding relationship with them allowed him to ask them to buy more than they usually would. He'd told them that he needed to move the product fast and since he'd probably made each of the men rich, they agreed to help out. He took their money and flew to Houston to get the ten million to pay Diego, so he would release Rico. Time was ticking.

Black noticed that TeTe had called him back to back. He called her back right away.

"Babe, I need to see you right away." she said.

"Can it be tomorrow? I got a lot going on today?"

"You really need to see me. I have something to show you."

"Okay, but I can't stay long. Where are you?"

"I'm in Dunwoody. I'll text you the address."

"Okay."

An hour later Black entered the house in Dunwoody. TeTe approached him and hugged him. Then she ordered him to follow her. He trailed her into a bedroom in the back of the house and when Black spotted the man with the Desert Eagle, he reached for his gun.

TeTe grabbed his hand and said, "Relax, baby. It's all right."

Black saw three men tied up, lying face down on the floor.

"What the hell is going on?"

"These are the men responsible for shooting the car."

Black recognized Mike, Tater and ugly-ass Kenny-Boo. He was confused. How did she know? How did she find them? How did she catch them? How did she bring them here? So many questions ran though his mind.

She slid her hands around Black's waist and said, "Mike?"

He looked up at Black, thinking that he knew Black was the motherfucker responsible for this. Black had murdered his brother and he'd thought that he would get a chance to avenge his brother's death but instead Black now had the upper hand.

"Untie him."

Black eyeballed Mike the whole time, wondering how she found them. He wanted to slap the fuck out of him with his crutch as soon as he saw the punk motherfucker.

"What are you going to do with these clowns?" Black asked.

TeTe stared at Black like he was a goddamned fool. "What do you think I'm going to do with them? What did they try to do to us?"

"You're going to kill them? Right now?"

"What do you think?"

"In this house?"

"Right now?"

Dank handed TeTe the pink 9.mm with a silencer. She approached Kenny-Boo and Tater then fired shots in the backs of their heads. Bullets ripped through their brains and blood spilled onto the floor.

Black starred in disbelief. He'd seen a lot of men die, but never had he known a bitch that was so ruthless. She approached Black and kissed him.

Mike was still bowing to her looking like a goddamned idiot. Happy that she'd spared him. She kept her promise and he was grateful and sad at the same time. Grateful that he was still living and disturbed that he'd watched his friends get murdered.

TeTe presented.Mike the picture of his son again, the same one of him sitting on the sofa. Then she shot him in the side of his head.

Black said, "You're a cold bitch."

"You didn't know?"

"I know now."

"And Shakur is next."

"What do you mean?"

"I know where he works out."

She wrapped her arms around him and led him into the next bedroom. She kicked her Louboutins off, laid her purse on the bed and unbuckled his belt. Black removed his shirt and was now in his wife-beater. The remote control to the surround sound was lying on the nightstand. She turned it on and Rick Ross and K Michelle's "If They Knew" blasted through the speakers.

TeTe kneeled before Black and said, "You ain't never met nobody like me and you never will." Then she took Black in her mouth.

Black believed her. He was attracted and afraid of her at the same time. Something about TeTe wasn't quite right. He knew he had to be careful. She was undeniable dangerous and sexy. She grabbed his hand and placed it on the back of her head.

"What are you doing?"

She laughed and said, "I don't usually like to suck dick, but I want to suck yours. Force feed it to me."

Black said, "This is crazy. You just murdered three motherfuckers and you want to fuck?"

"Why not?"

Black inserted his dick back into her mouth and placed his hand on the back of her head like she wanted and then force fed her his dick.

• • •

Q had flown first class to Houston to give the cholos the money and had gotten back to Atlanta the night before. Starr had dropped T.J. off at Trey's mother's house and came over to spend the night. She was still asleep when the phone buzzed. Q grabbed his iPhone. Eric, his distributer from North Carolina, had been calling back to back. And he saw that he had twenty-two text messages—all from his distributors.

He stepped into the guest bedroom down the hall and called Eric back. "What's up, E?"

"Bruh, this shit you sold me was a bad batch."

"What do you mean?"

"Dude, this shit was sheetrock mixed with coke."

"What?"

"I swear to God."

"Okay, I'll make it right."

"Okay."

"Was all of them like that?"

"All of them were fucked up pretty bad."

"What the fuck?"

"I ain't shitting you, bruh."

Q had always known Eric to be honest. He called all of his distributors and they all said the same thing.

Q called Diego. He didn't pick up.

Q received a call from the building concierge telling him he had a package. He told the concierge to send it up. The doorbell rang and Q made his way to the door. He looked through the peephole and saw it was a FedEx delivery.

Q opened the door and the deliveryman passed Q a box. The box came from Brownsville Texas. Q knew Brownsville was down by the Mexican border. He'd been there a few times with Diego. He took the package to the guest room and used a knife to cut into the box. The package was double-boxed. Q ripped into the second box.

He screamed when he saw Rico's head inside—eyes wide open, the gray streak of hair down his head like a skunk. The locket with the picture of his daughter Ivy still around his neck. Q removed the locket. That goddamned Diego had reneged on the deal and on top of that, he'd sent him bad dope. Not only had Diego murdered his friend, but Q had lost a shit load of money.

Starr banged on the door, and Q quickly closed the box.

"Come in."

"I thought I heard a scream."

"It was the TV."

Starr glanced at the plasma TV hanging over the desk. It wasn't on.

"I powered it down."

Starr eyed him suspiciously. "What's wrong, baby? You look like you've just left a haunted house." She laughed until she saw that he wasn't smiling.

There was an awkward silence then finally he said, "You have no idea."

To be continued ...

GET A FREE eBOOK!

Enjoyed this book?
If you enjoyed this book please write a review and email it to me at kevinelliott3@gmail.com, and get a FREE ebook.

K. Elliott Book Order Form

PO Box 12714
Charlotte NC 28220

Book Name	Quantity	Price	Shipping/ Handling	Total
Dear Summer		X $14.95	+ $3.00 per book	
Dilemma		X $14.95	+ $3.00 per book	
Entangled		X $13.95	+ $3.00 per book	
Godsend Series 1–5		X $14.95	+ $3.00 per book	
Godsend Series 6–10		X $14.95	+ $3.00 per book	
Kingpin Wifeys Vol. 1		X $14.95	+ $3.00 per book	
Kingpin Wifeys Vol. 2		X $14.95	+ $3.00 per book	
Kingpin Wifeys Vol. 3		X $14.95	+ $3.00 per book	
Kingpin Wifeys Vol. 4		X $14.95	+ $3.00 per book	
Kingpin Wifeys Vol. 5		X $14.95	+ $3.00 per book	
Kingpin Wifeys Vol. 6		X $14.95	+ $3.00 per book	
Street Fame		X $14.95	+ $3.00 per book	
Treasure Hunter		X $15.00	+ $3.00 per book	
			TOTAL	

Mailing Address

Name:

Mailing Address:

City	State	Zip

Method Of Payment

[ ] Check [ ] Money Order

Thank you for your support

About the Author

K. Elliott, aka The Well Fed Black Writer, penned his first novel, Entangled, in 2003. Although he was offered multiple signing deals, Elliott decided to found his own publishing company, Urban Lifestyle Press.

Bookstore by bookstore, street vendor by street vendor, Elliott took to the road selling his story. He did not go unnoticed, selling 50,000 units in his first year and earning a spot on the Essence Magazine Bestsellers list.

Since Entangled, Elliott has published five titles of his own and two more on behalf of authors signed to Urban Lifestyle Press. For one book, The Ski Mask Way, Elliott was selected to co-author with hip-hop superstar 50 Cent. Along the way, he has continued to look for innovative ways to push his books to his fans while keeping down his overhead.

Elliott is passionate about sharing what he has learned with aspiring authors, and has conducted learning webinars filled with information on what works best for him. He is the author of numerous best-sellers including Dilemma, Street Fame, Treasure Hunter, Dear Summer, Entangled, The Godsend Series and the hugely intriguing Kingpin Wifeys Series.